# Birds of Paradise

## Helen Pereira

Also by Helen Pereira:
Magpie in the Tower
*Creative Publishers, 1990*
The Home We Leave Behind
*Killick Press, 1992*
Wild Cotton
*Killick Press, 1994*

# Birds of Paradise

Helen Pereira

Killick Press
St. John's, Nowfoundland
1997

THE CANADA COUNCIL | LE CONSEIL DES ARTS
FOR THE ARTS | DU CANADA
SINCE 1957 | DEPUIS 1957

We acknowledge the support of the Canada Council for the Arts
for our publishing program

Cover photo: Michael Thomas

Published by
KILLICK PRESS
a Creative Book Publishing imprint
A Robinson-Blackmore Printing & Publishing associated company
P.O. Box 8660, St. John's, Newfoundland A1B 3T7

Printed in Canada by:
ROBINSON-BLACKMORE PRINTING & PUBLISHING

Canadian Cataloguing in Publication Data

Pereira, Helen, 1926-

Birds of paradise
ISBN 1-895387-79-5

I. Title

PS8581.E648B57   1997        C813'.54        C97-950087-7
PR9199.3.P428B57   1997

*For Stephen*

# Contents

Apartment Hunting _ _ _ _ _ _ _ _ _ _ _ _ _ _ _ _ _ _ _ 1

Birds of Paradise _ _ _ _ _ _ _ _ _ _ _ _ _ _ _ _ _ _ _ _ 15

Union Station _ _ _ _ _ _ _ _ _ _ _ _ _ _ _ _ _ _ _ _ _ 33

Osfa and The Canadian Mosaic _ _ _ _ _ _ _ _ _ _ _ _ 37

Guilt Trips _ _ _ _ _ _ _ _ _ _ _ _ _ _ _ _ _ _ _ _ _ _ 49

The Kettle Valley Celebrations
    The Golden Jubilee: 1947 _ _ _ _ _ _ _ _ _ _ _ _ _ _ 61

    The Centennial: 1997 _ _ _ _ _ _ _ _ _ _ _ _ _ _ _ 105

$\mathcal{T}$he Author wishes to thank Patricia Snider Armstrong and Faye Ode for editing early drafts; Lorraine Kelley and Bill Roedde for their encouragement; Shirley Murray and Peggy Phillips for clippings and photographs; and Koozma Tarasoff and John Popoff for photographs.

Two of these stories appeared in different versions elsewhere — 'Osfa and the Canadian Mosaic' in *Storyteller*, and 'Guilt Trips' in *The Texas Thoroughbred*.

Doukhobor choir photo, page 64: Koozma Tarasoff collection.

# Apartment Hunting

*P*amela finishes her breakfast — low-fat cottage cheese with a chopped banana half and a sprinkle of wheat germ; one slice of dry whole wheat toast. She leaves the kitchen table, takes her dishes to the sink, rinses them under the hot water tap, and sets them on the rack to dry.

Looking at the kitchen clock she exclaims, "It's already seven!" Pamela describes herself as 'a morning person' because she awakens between 4:30 and 5 a.m. On principle she lies on the sofa-bed listening to classical music on her headset until the station plays *O Canada* at 6. It's her private joke, arising to the national anthem.

She pours the last of the four large mugs of strong French Roast coffee she allows herself each morning, and to it, adds skim milk she makes from powder. She switched to a low-fat diet after her doctor's warnings about high cholesterol.

———

She carries her mug to the living room and settles down in the big easy chair. She sips her coffee, savours it: accus-

1

tomed now to the skim milk. She finishes half of it before picking up Saturday's *Globe and Mail*.

Aloud she asks, "What shall I treat myself to first?" Meaning the book section or the Cryptic Crossword, but decides, aloud again, "Neither."

She craves adventure, so hoards her favourite newspaper features for an evening indulgence with decaf, after she returns from an outing. Where to, she wonders, sliding out the classified section, then picking up glasses dangling from a thin chain around her neck. The chain became a necessity when she increasingly forgot where she put her reading glasses. She flips her way towards APARTMENTS, UNFURNISHED.

She smirks, whisking past COMPANIONS, PERSONAL, where her friends Sue and Vicky search for dates in the 'Young at Heart' segment.

Sue and Vicky giggle over their dates — how the men lie about their ages and occupations. Those claiming to be 'fit and fifty' are usually seniors on their last legs; those described as 'professional, retired,' turn out to be pensioners or unemployed loners, looking for free housekeeping and nursing care. *The poor souls.* Pamela frets at the very idea of her women friends lowering themselves by responding to ads when they have so much going for them. Degrees, not bad looks, teachers' pensions. Pamela warned them, shuddering, 'I worry about you two girls ending up in a ditch somewhere. Who knows what weirdos are out there?'

Pamela knows that she is safe because she has kept her pride, and because she does not have that desperate look Sue and Vicky acquired after dying their hair. Sue's a blatant black in a flapper bob; and Vicky's even worse, with her frizzy, nouveau-red perm. So old-looking, both of them.

Pamela is proud that not only does she not look her age, but that she is usually taken to be in her fifties, although approaching seventy.

She dresses as she always has: boldly and dramatically in big skirts, bright colours, wild earrings. She believes her students approve of her exotic streak and plays it up. What outfits she did not buy in foreign travel with her husband Gerald long ago, she adds to with purchases from Oxfam — proud to have kept her social conscience and her own hair colour. Highlighting is not the same as hair colouring, she explained to Sue and Vicky. 'I was always a natural blonde before my hair darkened.'

Her health and energy she attributes to exercise — a lifelong passion for swimming, and then in the seventies, when the fad started — to jogging, which she kept up until Gerald became ill with lung cancer and required so much care.

Her granddaughter Becky approves of Pamela's style. 'You look cool, Nana,' she'll say, when they dress to go out. Becky is studying political science at York University and lives in residence there, but occasionally spends weekends with Pamela out in Burlington.

They attend movies, plays, art shows: Fridays they order in fish-and-chips or pizza. At least, on those increasingly infrequent weekends when Becky visits because she has a big laundry and ironing to do, or needs to use Pamela's computer. When her grandmother phones to make arrangements for a weekend, Becky is often busy with meetings, demonstrations, or just hanging out with foreign students. Such 'attitude' Becky has! What was called 'pizzazz' in Pamela's day.

She pumps Becky about campus life, remembering her

own early university years. *Latin-American Club, Debating Society. Nearly flunked my first year.*

The two of them do get along, even though Becky teases her grandmother about talking to herself.

'It's just habit,' Pamela explained. 'I used to talk to my cat Sandy all the time, that's all.'

Becky also teases her about the magazine photos of Paul Newman and Sean Connery taped to the refrigerator. Newman's face was defended by Pamela because of his charitable work: Connery's because of his support of Scottish Nationalism. 'We're Scots, you know, Becky.'

'Give me a break, Nana,' Becky snapped. 'Those guys are there because you've got the hots for them. They're vintage hunks!'

Pamela giggled and owned, 'They are handsome men. I'll agree to that. But, Becky dear, they are both married.'

Pamela finishes her coffee, sets her cup on the bookcase, and runs her hand firmly along the newspaper's edge. She frowns at the black blur left on her fingers by the printers' ink, and inwardly complains, What is wrong with newspapers nowadays? She purses her mouth with distaste at the smudgy feeling, but continues to finger the column. Searching. Where to this week?

She avoids the obituary column, although drawn to it. She avoids it because seeing the name of a friend, colleague or acquaintance there, throws her into a black mood. A mood only dispelled by walking, walking, walking, until elation sets in, soon followed by fatigue so severe that she has to take a bus home. After the walk she is herself again; able to focus, grief dissipated. Able to mark papers, prepare lessons, clean up her apartment.

She boasts that she 'still has a life,' and stimulation from teaching English part-time, getting to meet young people and immigrants. Contacts which she believes have kept her flexible and open-minded. It is a sunny day, and ordinarily she would be out on the balcony preserving her tan. At least she kept the tan, she muses, remembering her disappointing Palm Beach vacation.

Pamela had prepared for weeks before leaving with tanning-parlour sessions so she wouldn't arrive looking pale and touristy. Palm Beach was a let-down, after all her anticipated excitement and fun. She expected so much after making such an effort with her appearance — even joining Weight Watchers until she was able to fit into a size ten, then rewarding herself by having her hair styled in a beauty salon, where a handsome young Italian persuaded her to also have it highlighted. She balked at first, remembering her lectures to Sue and Vicky, but when the stylist — Carmelo was his name— told her she 'looked too young at heart' not to 'go for it,' she gave in. Every morning she still feels surprised, looking in the mirror. She touches her hair and smiles.

When Becky saw her make-over she blurted, 'Wow, Nana! Are you off in search of a boyfriend?' Pamela smarted. Not because it was too close to the truth, but because Becky's giggle implied that the idea of her grandmother with 'a boyfriend' was funny.

In spite of Becky's words, Pamela had hoped to meet someone brilliant and interesting at Palm Beach. Perhaps someone like Dominick Dunne. Drinking mineral water together over literary chats. 'Now take Faulkner,' she'd begin, and imagine the silver-haired escort leaning forward, ready with his own literary interjection. That holiday was the most disappointing experience of her life. She'd chosen a hotel near the airport because she thought business executives would be vacationing there, but upon arrival found that all the guests were just plain busy, not vacationing. The hotel staff was cold and unfriendly, even though she tipped generously. Worse still, the pool was unheated, so only Pamela used it. There was no laughing crowd gathering around after a plunge, socializing over drinks. Accustomed to cold water she determinedly swam alone, thinking she was asserting her superior Canadian circulatory system while worrying that her athleticism created an impression of eccentricity. 'Eccentric' was fine for foreign students, but not for conservative executives at an upscale American hotel. She held her ground; refused to waste her tan, her new Speedo bathing suit, her patriotism. She continued swimming lengths until one day coming out of the pool she looked up and saw a couple peering through the glass door, watching her and giggling.

She was glad to get back to Toronto.

---

"Where was I?" she asks aloud, meaning, her own thoughts. "Oh yes. Flexible and open-minded. Where to today?"

She searches the page for an interesting destination for her afternoon outing. She finds one. The Beaches. Perfect.

Last Saturday her trip to an Etobicoke condo was disappointing. The manager was brusque and there were no other interesting people out looking. Not the sort of people Pamela enjoyed engaging in friendly conversation — like that Somalian family she met once, or those exotic Salvadorean refugees she spoke to on another visit. No, just a boring young newlywed couple holding hands. It hadn't been worth dressing up. If today's apartment search is a letdown, she decides, she will walk along the boardwalk and stop for lunch at some trendy little restaurant.

She does not need a new apartment. Her own apartment is actually quite pleasant and she has just renewed her lease as she always does. There's a gym, a pool, good security and reasonable rent.

Apartment living is new to her, but she likes it, although she had lived in her own home right up until Gerald died.

When he was diagnosed with lung cancer she was torn between fury and grief. Fury, because she blamed his smoking: grief because she loved him. They had children. And she was, well, used to him. Used to him. She reflects on the syntax of that phrase, thinks of it as, 'to his use.' Of course.

During his illness and long dying it was painful watching him waste away. Waste. Away. It was then she gained weight herself, as if eating to strengthen him.

She hung on in their Riverdale home, much to the distress of her daughters Liz and Carolyn; who, although shattered by their own grief, warned her that the house would tie her down, would depress her with memories.

'You've got to move,' they urged.

'No,' she retorted. 'It's my life. You grew up here.'

She stubbornly resisted until several months later, when her daughters informed her of their plan to teach in Zambia with their husbands.

That did it. She would just show them. She sold the house. Parted with furniture, garden, everything. She too, could move on.

She did. Back to university for her Master's degree and into a small studio apartment in Ann Arbor. To her astonished friends, she explained, 'Women don't own houses. Houses own them.'

Her apartment in Michigan, and the one in Burlington, were both friendly in the sense of tenants speaking to each other in corridors or on elevators, but Pamela believes it unwise to get too friendly in the visiting sense. In apartments that sort of thing could get out of hand. The first thing she knew people would be knocking on her door and dropping in all the time and she'd have no privacy.

Not that she minds it when Michel, the nice Montreal lad who rents her parking space, drops by with his monthly cheque. After he responded to her sign on the laundromat notice board she bought a wine rack, one of those really good corkscrews, and some nice French and German wines. Now, when Michel arrives at the first of the month she invites him to have a drink: lets him open the bottle and pour the wine the way she would with a lover or a mate. They chat until the bottle is finished.

Michel is tall and blond and is studying business administration at the University of Toronto. He doesn't look French at all. Pamela enjoys their political talk, and especially enjoys Michel, who is a passionate Quebecois. Pamela is convinced he stays, not out of politeness, nor because of the wine, but because he, too, enjoys their conversations. It is, however, always Michel who finishes the bottle. Pamela has learned that at her age even very good wines upset her stomach and disturb her sleep. But Michel is young, big: and, well, the French are accustomed to drinking gracefully.

In the classifieds she spots a two-bedroom with solarium, en suite laundry, and cable. Perfect. The sort of place that might attract an interesting tenant. Perhaps a widower — a writer who would use the second bedroom for his office. Yes! She flings the paper down, looks across the room and admires the bleached ash coffee table in front of her sofa. A recent acquisition, like everything else. She smiles, remembering what a time she and Becky had getting everything assembled. All those screwdrivers, diagrams, and directions in Swedish.

She considers the sofa-bed, really too large for the apartment, which she bought hoping for overnight visitors. Children, grandchildren, lively colleagues. But her daughters and their husbands are off in Africa, and her Michigan friends have scattered. To Alaska, Texas, Florida — or else committed to completing their Ph.D's. So far, except for Becky, only Pamela herself sleeps on the sofa, falling asleep on it nightly, watching TV. She finds it easy to drop off in the living room, and is irritated and confused when awakened by some raucous infomercial — a signal to drag herself into the bedroom. There, in the space designated for sleep, she lies tossing about, finally returning to the living room, the sofa, TV, and sleep. It's cognitive dissonance, that's all, she tells herself. Being able to sleep where sleep is not expected.

---

She strides into the bathroom and takes off her tracksuit — a comfy old outfit she slops around in. When it falls on the bathroom floor, she kicks it aside with her foot.

She takes a bottle of green apple bath oil from the bathroom shelf, measures a capful into the tub, turns on both hot and cold water taps until the temperature feels just right before she climbs carefully into the scented warmth. Then she settles down and sighs with pleasure. She wriggles her tense shoulders in frothy water, enjoys the sensation, the swishing sounds. Relaxed, she leans back, and happily wonders what to wear today. Her favourite Mexican embroidered skirt and blouse? With the dangly silver earrings?

---

She'd worn that outfit on one of her most successful hunts. A very promising encounter. At a High Park condo. After the usual inquiries to the resident manager — a pleasant Pole — she was leaving with an application and her practised comment about 'going home to think it over.'

At the exit she was overtaken by a tall, silver-haired man carrying a load of books, a load so cumbersome she was about to open the door for him. Instead, he pushed ahead to hold the door for her.

"Hope I'm not offending any feminist principles," he said, grinning. "It's just that old habits die hard."

"Not at all, thank you," she mumbled. "You're the one carrying the load. It seems more sensible for me to hold the door for you."

He smiled, looking her over, she noticed, particularly observing her Mexican garb, as he said, "I gave up on being sensible long ago."

His comment, amused blue eyes, and apparent approval of her costume unnerved her. She was always shy with attractive men. When she scanned his book titles and saw two of her favourites — William Trevor and Paul Theroux — it was too much. She flushed, quickened her pace and moved ahead of him.

"Are you a new tenant?" he asked breezily, catching up to her with long strides.

"No. Just looking. Apartment hunting."

"I'm off to the library," he explained. "It's right around the corner."

When they reached the subway she knew she must leave, but was unable to comment on his books, tongue-tied at meeting an attractive man with tastes similar to hers. She muttered, "Well, goodbye."

"Goodbye," he responded. "Perhaps I'll see you again if you decide on an apartment here."

She smiled to herself all the way to Burlington on the GO train: for weeks imagined living in that building. Imagined their growing friendship. Little dinner parties with his friends. She thought of him as an engineer — a civil engineer like Gerald. His friends might be engineers also, or academics. Retired professors — perhaps from a Spanish department — with whom she could practise Spanish and discuss her travels. They might even share their views about Canary Island resorts, Barcelona architecture, Cuban and Central American politics.

In the tub she considers more open responses she might have made to the silver-haired engineer. 'Could you show me the library? I might as well check it out.' Or, 'I'm a Trevor fan myself. Did you hear him at Harbourfront?'

———————

But she had been unable to say those things. Why? she wonders, scrubbing her body with a loofah.

I've always felt it was important to keep my skin smooth. Gerald liked that.

She lingers in diminishing bubbles before reaching for a bottle of camomile shampoo on the tub's edge. She lathers and rinses her hair twice: ends with a cool rinse under the shower. Carmelo told her that a cool rinse brought out the shine.

Very cautiously she reaches for the towel rack, to balance herself as she rises from the tub. Caution is new to her. She winces; remembers that incident back in Michigan when she slipped and cracked her elbow on the tub edge, remembers the long agonizing slither across the tile, across the broadloom, the effort of getting into bed. Fortunately she always kept a glass of water and inflammatory tablets beside her bed. She'd gulped down three tablets but lay awake all night in agony.

She convinced herself it was just a sprain. From her running days she recalled RICE — rest, ice, compression, elevation —and managed to make her way to the fridge, bracing her injured elbow against her side while with her free arm, she withdrew a package of frozen strawberries. Back in bed she propped her arm on the cold plastic bundle and moaned all night while reminding herself, tomorrow is Saturday. It will be alright, the pain will ease up.

It did not.

Monday she arrived at university by bus in a Tylenol-haze wearing a long-sleeved dress, presenting herself for her final oral examination. Chaucer / Shakespeare / Hopkins /Frost /Curtal Sonnets / Spenserian sonnets / enjambment / sprung rhythm / tragic flaws / alienation and God-only-knows-what. Afterwards, she held her arm tightly, hurried away rudely while her professors congratulated her.

She picked her steps carefully to the health centre because everything was becoming blurry and she was afraid of fainting on the street. The nurse-practitioner at the centre commended her for doing the right things — ice, tablets — but chastised her for not having gone to emergency immediately. A doctor was summoned, an x-ray taken, and an ulnar fracture diagnosed. Surgery was ordered. "No," Pamela said through gritted teeth. "I'm flying home. To Toronto. Please call me a cab." The nurse protested but complied after the doctor nodded, murmuring, "No insurance. They have medicare."

Pamela returned to her apartment, dumped her books, grabbed her purse, and headed for the airport home to Canada, medicare, and Mount Sinai hospital.

There, finally, she let go and sobbed. At all the pain and bravado she'd gone through alone. She did not smile when the jocular resident told her she was 'a tough old bird,' Although later, trembling, she clutched his hand in the O.R. before the anaesthetic. Fearing the mini-death: the rehearsal.

After surgery and a short rest at Sue's, she returned to Ann Arbor with a cast and a smile to await her commencement ceremony.

───────

She wraps one towel around her head, dries herself with another before slathering herself with Oscar de la Renta body lotion and spraying her breasts with Oscar cologne. From the bathroom door hook she takes her aqua-green terry robe bought for the Palm Beach pool. She worries again. What to wear?

───────

Barefoot she pads into her room, slides open the closet door to view her wardrobe: pauses before the Mexican outfit. She lifts its wild embroidered skirt from the hanger along with the matching blouse.

This will look super with my tan, she thinks. All those bright colours.

At first she'd enjoyed the tanning parlour, looked forward to lying nude in the tanning bed's warmth, dreaming of Palm Beach. She would continue with these sessions, she decided, aware she looked better tanned. Until one day another client emerged from a cubicle shuddering, 'Never again! When the top slides down above me it's like being in a coffin.' Pamela was standing at the counter signing out when she heard that, and shivered. She never went back.

She pauses, fingers her favourite skirt, considers it. Gerald bought it for her on their last trip. She returns her Mexican costume to the hanger, places it far back in the closet.

She wants something different, something new, and smiles at the sight of a handwoven peacock-blue Zambian dress. It has a low neckline outlined with heavy white crocheted lace. She loves this costume so much that she saved it. For what? When? It was a present from one of her daughters. From which one? To the cupboard she announces, "It was from Liz!"

She grabs the dress from the hanger.

Yes, this is what I'll wear today. Something new and exciting.

Something bold.

# Birds of Paradise

The bird of paradise stems are brittle in the long crystal vase: their purple and orange buds have yet to open. Emma changes the water, trims the stems, mists the week-old bouquet, and awaits the ultimate purple thrust. A fern frond in the arrangement is still green, but she'd discarded the yellow rosebud that bloomed overnight, showering petals across her coffee table. When roses go, they go. That's it. The bird of paradise flowers, however, hold colour and structure. Make a promise.

She takes off her glasses and gives up on a pile of essays she was word-processing for clients — part-time work she began after retirement from teaching. But her work has been typo-riddled ever since Salim entered her life.

She wanders into the kitchen to admire all the fruit: oranges, persimmons, kiwis; picks up a pomegranate, caresses its red skin and returns it to the fruit bowl.

She takes a goblet down from the cupboard, fills it with water, and to it adds a drop of orange blossom essence that came with Salim's gifts: the bouquet and fruit-filled basket;

the bags of hummus, babaganoush, halvah. She smiles at the bottle's label — the curly Arabic script — before she replaces it on her spice and flavouring shelf.

She turns on the answering machine and takes her drink to the bedroom. There must be no disturbances while she centres herself in meditation.

Sipping flavoured water, she wonders, which incense to use? Sandalwood, she decides. She sets down her drink, lights a stick in a brass holder before darting back into the living room to insert a CD of 'The Three Tenors' in her player.

After undressing, she hangs up her jeans and sweatshirt. She has resolved to change, to become neater for Salim, and to stop tossing stuff on the floor. She changes into a loose track suit she reserves for meditation, slips off her worn-out Ojibwa moccasins and steps onto the new raspberry-coloured prayer mat, slithering rough bunioned feet across its plush finish. Finally she stretches out on her back in relaxation position: legs apart, arms outstretched. Begins deep breathing.

Inhale positive .... one ... two .. three .. four ..

Exhale negative .... one ... two .. three .. four ..

Floats, floats, to voices of tenors she calls 'my three Latins.'

Placido. *Ô Paradis!*

...*Pays merveilleux, jardin fortune, Temple radieux, salut...*

Her tenors have been faithful: caused no trouble except in her fantasies. If she had to choose, which one? Luciano? Jose? Placido? She favours Luciano but loathes cooking Italian food. The messy sauces. She enjoys fantasies, lets herself go with them, breathing.

...*O paradis sorti de l'onde...*

Inhale positive .... one .... two ... three .. four ..

Exhale negative .... one .... two ... three .. four ..
Placido's words waft in sandlewood-scented air.
...*Monde nouveau, tu m'appartiens...Sois donc a moi!*...
Hormone surges disrupt her. Tonight, neither medita-
tion nor her tenors soothe. Sleep is frightening because of a
recent dream she had, because of its amazing consequences.
The actual arrival of Salim. Why had he entered her life?
Why, after she had just settled in her Mississauga apartment?
The move had been prudent, given her recent retirement
from teaching — but scary and upsetting. As she quipped to
her daughter April, 'It's my last move before the anatomy
lab.'

She soon came to enjoy her new surroundings — parks,
lake, cafes — until that night, tired and disoriented, she slept
deeply.

---

She dreamed she stood outside her former apartment in
a group with her ex-husband Ken, who usually starred in her
many troubled dreams. In this special dream he was unim-
portant, so compelled was she to discover who occupied her
former space.

The door left ajar tempted. What excuse to give? Items
forgotten? Mail unforwarded? She stalled. Two of her poet
clients, Megan and Beth, arrived clad in mini-dresses and
what looked like army boots with heels. 'Go on in, Emma,'
they coaxed, 'Don't be a fraidy cat.'

She tiptoed inside: her former apartment was now deco-
rated with oriental rugs and huge floor pillows, and in it were
two short, dark men. Both wore scarlet fezzes and silken
scarlet shirts; purple trousers. One of them sat in a carved
wooden chair, his back to the door beside a mirrored wall, his

head bowed and hands clasped. Bergamot scent drifted from an incense stick in a brass holder on a small table at his side. She halted, dazzled. This sight was like an illustration from *The Arabian Nights*.

Another man stood on the far side of the room holding an exotic stringed instrument. He laid it on a satin pillow, made salaam, and urged, 'Come in! Come in!'

She waited. After the prayerful man made the greeting salaam she told him, 'I'm sorry if I disturbed your meditation.'

He did not reply but his black eyes shone a welcome. The other man repeated, 'Come in!'

She awoke so excited that she phoned Megan — not only had Megan appeared in the dream, but in real life was in Jungian therapy.

'Amazing!' Megan enthused. 'You're finally leaving your repressive husband behind. Those exotic men are new animus figures, freeing your sensual self.'

Feeling no magic click from Megan's words, Emma sought a second opinion from Elise, a writer of metaphysical articles.

Elise lifted an elegant hand to her forehead and said, "Colours... in my life... precede rebirth... I had similar dreams... after my six children were grown... I left my husband... bought a red jump suit... highlighted my hair... flew to a charismatic symposium in Dublin... oh, the glorious dancing priests..." A smile flickered around her lips. "I felt quite the scarlet woman."

"Elise? Elise? My dream? What about my dream?"

"Oh... your dream... spiritual renewal... it goes with aging... moving..."

Emma was disappointed. She wanted to return to her

own wonderful dream and get to know those exotic men. Especially the silent one.

Megan once told her a person could control their dreams by concentrating on the desired subject before retiring. Emma tried this. At bedtime she gulped *The Rubaiyat*, nibbled *The Koran*, devoured *The Arabian Nights*. No luck.

---

A week later, although she hated poetry readings, Emma prepared to attend Megan's. "You must come," Megan had begged. "You alone know my psyche, went through book birth pangs with me. You're my poetic midwife. Besides, poetry is vital to you at this time, because dreams and poetry are related."

"Well, okay. I'll ask Elise. She'll come."

"Sorry," Elise said, "I cannot... invited to a seance... copy for a New Age magazine... I'm wearing my purple kaftan... Or do you think a silver lycra jump suit more appropriate?"

"For a seance, definitely purple. But if you don't go to the reading, neither will I."

"Oh... poetry... you must go... your dream... an omen..."

Emma dressed and recalled how often she'd set out for Bread and Bards cafe before. Hoping to snag new clients, hoping for good wine and canapes, while loathing an ambience at what she regarded to be a literati singles' club. She'd dressed, done her hair, and so often been disappointed that she'd usually given up, changed into Ken's old plaid dressing gown, and stayed home with her tenors.

Damn Megan and Elise, she thought, blow-drying her hair and applying makeup. She put on her brown gabardine suit and looked in the mirror. Too *brown*. She'd have stayed home if it were not such a mellow Indian summer evening, a warm and beautiful night. She flung off the suit and strode to her closet. She knew what to wear! A three-piece silk outfit April had given her. Its bronze camisole was worn with a loose jacket and floaty divided skirt of purple, pink and orange print. Emma had wondered when she'd ever wear it. Tonight! Its colours matched the autumn sky. She slid into her new apparel and admired herself in the mirror.

Awaiting the bus she watched sky colours deepen, unaware of the bus stopping until the driver yelled, "Are you getting in or what?"

Startled, she leapt on, blurted, "Sorry."

She arrived at Bread and Bards early; slipped past students pretending to study, writers pretending to write, aware that soon she'd be pretending to enjoy the reading. She slunk into the washroom, looked in the mirror, again admired her outfit — its colours, its silky feeling. A change from the severe suits she'd worn to look professional when teaching. She tried the jacket buttoned and unbuttoned, but left it unbuttoned, because she liked the way the camisole showed off her tan. She reapplied lipstick and approved of her eye makeup.

She glanced at her watch: 8:15. Striving to look casual, she sauntered into the cafe, searched for an empty table, awaiting Megan's effusive hug. Nothing. She looked at the side where table and chairs were usually set for guest readers. Her eyes widened: her mouth opened.

There was her Arabian dream man: hands before him, palms together. Also the other man, who set down his stringed instrument, salaamed and urged, "Come in! Come in!" Both wore the same exotic costumes they had in her dream. Emma stood shocked. The solemn man made salaam. His black eyes shone a welcome. *I am in Bread and Bards, not in a dream. This is real. Those are real students and writers.* She grabbed a chair beside a young couple and whispered, "Where's Megan Tompkins?" "Stormed off in a huff. That's Salim, the famous ghazal poet from Bahrain. What a treat! I'm seriously into ghazals. Salim reads at Harbourfront tomorrow, but he knows the cafe owners, so while he's in town he's also reading here. Tompkins fumed over being dumped, blaming someone called Emma. Good riddance! This is special."

"It's special to me," Emma said. "I'm staying. Do you want anything? I'm desperate for coffee."

"No. We're cool for now. Besides, we only drink camomile tea. You go ahead, we'll keep your seat for you."

"Thanks." As Emma ordered a *latte*, the poet signalled the attendant. She was astonished when the waiter placed a tiny cup and copper pot on a tray and said, "Turkish coffee. From Salim."

I'll stumble for sure, she thought, smiling at the two men. Salim remained meditative. His companion again made salaam while the audience stared. She tiptoed to the table and set down her tray. When she tasted her coffee, the caffeine hit. Emma was a gulper, but the strength of this new brew forced her to savour tiny sips.

"We never knew they had Turkish coffee," the camomile couple complained, rushing to the counter. When others saw and followed, a waiter shook his head. Customers trailed back to their tables: some settled for refills of *lattes* and *au laits*.

The camomile couple rose, put on their coats, and, scowling at Emma, headed out. When the musician announced that the reading was to begin, and that Salim, aware of his academic audience, would read in Urdu, the couple returned. The wife commented, "That's more like it. Ghazals don't work in translation." Some people groaned and left: others whispered appreciatively.

This must be an Urdu crowd, Emma thought, dislodging coffee grounds from a back tooth.

The speaker continued, "Because of the learned nature of this audience, I need not explain the ghazal form and conventions."

Salim rose, faced Emma, and recited to her while his partner strummed his instrument. The camomile people shoved closer: Emma's sudden friends.

"I love the oud," the woman whispered. "My husband Tom prefers the santoor. I believe the oud to be the superior ghazal accompaniment."

As she listened to the poet, Emma was amazed. She'd never studied Urdu, but somehow understood it: from the foreign instrument heard familiar sounds. But she blushed. Such erotic poems!

At intermission people thumbed through Salim's books. Others discussed the oud with the musician. When the waiter brought Emma a note, she held it away from the couple peeking over her shoulder.

She read: PLEASE HONOUR US BY ACCOMPANYING
US TO OUR SUITE.
SALIM WILL PREPARE A MIDDLE EASTERN MEAL
FOR YOU.

No formal acceptance was expected. Salim knew she

would accept, just as she knew her dream had prepared her to meet him.

The second half of the performance was similar to the first, although more of the audience left. The non-Urdu crowd, she supposed. A reporter from *Books in Canada* gave her his card and asked for an interview. She ignored him, captivated by Salim wooing her in an ancient tradition.

After the reading the cafe owner offered to introduce her to Salim.

"There's no need," Emma replied. "We've already met."

Salim nodded and Emma explained, "In a dream."

"In that case," the owner said, "there's no problem."

Salim presented her to his brother, Sarif, and helped her into the jacket she'd slipped off at intermission. "Your divided skirt is like harem pants worn by our Middle Eastern women," he commented.

"If I may say so," she said, "I admire your clothes. Western men's clothes are boring."

"Indeed," Salim responded. "We prefer our garments. They are also more appropriate for performance."

Departing, they shook hands with the owner, all making their farewells in Urdu.

———

Outside, they ushered her into a Hertz rental car. Salim sat beside her in the back while Sarif drove.

"Salim avoids talk," Sarif said, swerving onto the Gardiner Expressway. "He conserves energy for love, poetry, cooking."

Salim nodded. "Yes. And my brother saves his precious hands for the oud."

They sped into the underground parking lot, left the car

with a valet, and ushered her to an elevator that stopped at
the twenty-second floor. They welcomed her to their suite.
Her dream suite! The same thick rugs, floor pillows, and to
the right of the entrance, a carved wooden chair beside the
mirrored wall. On a small table, an incense stick in a brass
holder. She felt right at home.

As Salim headed for the kitchen she asked, "Do you
meditate?"

"Yes."

"Do you believe in synchronicity?"

"Of course. Would you like to play? I've 'The Jung Game'
on my computer. Sarif will show you how to use it while I
prepare dinner."

They led her to an oval room with a circular table that
held a computer and a fax machine. There was another
computer in the living room, a third in an alcove off the
kitchen — each tuned to a different Internet program. An old
movie on one, 'Oprah' on another, 'The Jung Game' on
another. A CD played Oriental music. Salim set her down in
front of 'The Jung Game.' She was confused.

"I'm not one for computers. I'd rather watch you cook,"
she said. "I love Middle Eastern food, and the CD. That's
exciting music."

"That's Sarif's latest. We'll give you one. He signed a new
contract when we were in New York. Middle Eastern music
has caught on here in the west the way ghazals did in the
seventies. Come then, and help me prepare dinner. Although
it is written that I must cook for you, you may practise while
awaiting my return."

At the counter he stirred tahini into hummus, scooped
fava beans and chick peas into crystal bowls. He sprinkled
cumin on the beans, commenting, "Cumin is great stuff."

"I know," she said. "I use it a lot."

Although she wondered what he'd meant by 'awaiting my return,' she was patient. Salim was her fate.

He handed her a bowl. "Let's put these out." They carried a variety of beans to a table covered by a white linen cloth and set with a tray of lettuce, cucumbers, and red peppers. A fruit tray displayed orange persimmons cut into stars, nestling near green kiwi slices. She caught her breath when Salim sprinkled pomegranate seeds on hummus, chopped parsley over beans.

"Salim, I give you an A+ for presentation."

"That good, eh?"

"I've never seen such a colourful meal! I haven't had pomegranates since I was a child. My father got them for us at Christmas."

Salim smiled. "Please sit down, Emma. Come, Sarif."

Sarif left his computer to join them.

They waited for her. She hesitated. Salim understood her confusion and explained, "We don't use forks or knives. Just our fingers. Like this." He tore some pita, scooped it in hummus and popped it into his mouth. "Go ahead."

She broke off a bit of pita, dipped it in babaganoush. She took another. And another. Scooped up beans and hummus, murmuring with pleasure.

"At first I didn't want to eat anything, you know? It all looked so beautiful. Everything is delicious." While she savoured the texture and pungency of pomegranate seeds in creamy hummus, the brothers watched and smiled.

Salim took a pitcher of ice water from the fridge, filled their glasses and to them added drops from a tiny bottle. He gave her a glass. "Try this."

Emma swished a mouthful, swallowed, and asked, "What is it? Sort of familiar, but different."

"Orange flower water. The blossom essence takes away the ho-hum from plain water."

"It sure does," she agreed. "Where did you get it?"

"From a local Middle Eastern store. We were surprised at the variety here in Toronto. We usually have to bring our own supplies when touring, but found all we needed right here."

"Yes," she agreed. "I have most of these foods at home."

While they ate and talked, Emma told them of her dream. She was disappointed when they saw nothing special about it.

"To dream of an event in advance simply means that it is written," Sarif explained. "What we call qasama, and you call kismet."

They chatted, sipping flavoured water, nibbling fruit. She enjoyed herself so much she was shocked when she noticed her watch. "It's past midnight! I'll clean up and call a cab."

"No, dear Emma." Salim said. "I clean up. I will do so after driving you home."

"I'm imposing on you both. You must be exhausted. The reading, the meal. It's all too much to expect."

He was already carrying plates to the sink. Sarif excused himself and sent a fax to his agent.

———————

Salim took her hand and led her to the elevator, then through the underground to his car. They set off for Mississauga along the Gardiner Expressway.

Emma trembled. Salim's presence excited her. Would they make love?

As if answering her thoughts, Salim said, "It is written that we will be lovers, but our magic will not come to pass until after my tour. It is now October. I will return for you in March, at winter's end and spring's beginning, when we will depart for our new life in Bahrain."

Emma worried. "Won't I see you before you leave?"

"Of course. After tomorrow's reading. Do not prepare food. I will bring everything."

At her apartment he parked outside, escorted her up in the elevator and to her door. He kissed her, and she pressed close to him. He moved away.

"We will meet tomorrow," he whispered, and departed. She fumbled for her key and opened her door. When she looked back Salim had vanished.

Aroused by their meeting, she tossed all night. What would Megan and Elise say if they knew of her experience? She would not tell them: she wanted to keep her tryst a secret, fearing that talk would destroy its magic. She also remembered what the camomile couple told her about Megan's reaction to being replaced by Salim.

---

It was chilly when she arose next morning, so she decided to make soup. Pea soup would warm Salim when he arrived. She chopped celery, onions, carrots, and garlic, added it to a pot of water and left it all to simmer with dried peas.

That afternoon she walked to work off her excitement. Had Salim meant what he said about waiting to become lovers?

Her thoughts were interrupted by honks of geese flying

south. Looking up, she wished Salim were with her to share this ultimate Canadian experience. She watched, thrilled as always, but wondered. Could she leave Canada? And how would she look wearing *abaya*? Am I being ridiculous? she wondered. I hardly know him. But I feel that I know him because I already met him in a dream.

She strode along the lakeshore. Mothers pushed tots in strollers and kids roared past on bikes. The further she walked, the warmer and more energetic she felt. She had a date! Returning, she slowed her pace to conserve energy.

---

She got busy straightening her apartment for Salim's visit, threw out newspapers, dusted bookcases, emptied garbage. She tidied the bedroom and changed her sheets and pillow cases.

When she returned to the kitchen, the soup was a thick puree. She ladled out a bowlful, turned off the heat, sat down and ate. Ambrosia! Salim would love it. Rinsing the bowl, she decided to wear her coral sweater, tights, and purple slippers. She was glad daily walks kept her slim enough for tights, and that she wore slippers because Salim was short. She styled her greying hair, repeating the effort with eye makeup she'd made the previous night. She wrapped a towel around her head and across her face to see how she'd look wearing an *abaya*. Pale. More eye-liner.

What about music? Salim might be threatened by her tenors. She chose the CD Sarif had given her. This new music would set the mood for her tryst with Salim: this music that made her want to dance.

Her excitement rose as time for Salim's arrival neared. She was reheating the soup when the intercom buzzed and she heard his voice call, "I'm here!"

"Come right up!"

It seemed hours before he knocked. Through the peephole she saw him carrying flowers and a huge basket. When she opened the door he reached across his bundles to kiss her. He handed her the bouquet, set down the basket, and looked around at her kitchen, exclaiming, "What a great colour! Hades Red. I love it."

"I'm glad. I needed a change after the move. How did you know the colour's name?"

"From my dream. You got the paint on sale at Sears."

"Amazing," she said. "So it *was* written."

"Of course." He shifted from one foot to the other, watching her unwrap the flowers. She gasped. There were two perfect bird of paradise buds, a yellow rosebud, and a fern frond.

"My favourite flower! I can't believe you knew!"

"Believe it, Emma," he replied. "That knowledge is also from *my* dream." He passed her a card and commanded, "Read it."

She squinted at his strange handwriting.

TO EMMA, MY LOVE FOREVER, SALIM.

She murmured, "...Gosh...that's so...I must take care of my flowers..." She scurried away to find a crystal vase. As she filled it with water, her hands shook. No man had ever courted her so lavishly. Or was it courtship?

Salim opened more parcels. Hummus, beans, falafels.

"These are still warm," he said, setting out falafels. "The lady at Aladdin's cafe just fried them for us."

"Open the other parcels," he coaxed. "I took advice from a Leonard Cohen song. Can you guess? But it's not tea."

She opened a box of Turkish coffee, a bag of oranges and responded," 'Suzanne By The River.' "

She was flattered that such a famous poet as Salim was so eager to please her, and by the way he watched her face while she opened each gift.

He stared at his feet. "I wanted to write you a new ghazal, but I don't write well on tour."

"Of course not," she said. "I understand."

Salim took over her kitchen and set the table exactly the way he had at his suite.

"Would you like soup first?" she asked.

"What kind?"

"Pea soup. To warm you up."

He went to the stove and lifted the lid. "This looks great! Let's have soup first."

When he sat at Emma's kitchen table and spread the napkin on his lap, he reminded her of April as a baby seated in a high chair awaiting pablum: that same anticipation and pleasure in being cared for. He ate two bowls of soup before tucking into falafels.

They discussed books. When she asked him his favourite poet, he said, "Ogden Nash."

She was surprised by his answer, but still seeking a common interest asked, "Do you like opera?"

"Opera?" He looked puzzled.

"You know. Music? What kind do you like?"

"Music from my own land. Our own sound. Some of our musicians espouse western technology, but Sarif is a purist.

We are from an ancient culture, the Earth's cradle. The oud is mother of all stringed instruments. The lute, guitar, et cetera. But I do admit to enjoying Leonard Cohen's songs. And The Beatles. We share the poet's soul. But I avoid western literature. I read only *The Koran*, Khayyam, and Rumi. In the original languages. I don't want to lose my voice."

Although disappointed that they shared so few interests, Emma remained positive. "I understand. I work as a word-processor for poets and writers. They're always going on about voice." She consoled herself with the thought that Salim was a serious dreamer and a marvellous cook. How much more could she ask?

When he volunteered to clean up after dinner, she objected. She offered him soup to take home, and he agreed. Watching her pour it into a plastic carton he said, "Don't forget Sarif. He loves soup, but it's too time-consuming for me to make when we're on tour."

She led him into her living room where they sat on a big couch before the coffee table on which she'd placed the bouquet.

"I want to enjoy my flowers," she explained, stroking a bird of paradise bud.

"It will bloom and grow more colourful," Salim asserted. "That is my promise."

They discussed religion, love, politics, and cooking. To demonstrate a point about cooking as art, Salim took a huge orange and pared it into the shape of a rose.

"You're amazing," she said. "I hack and peel. You make food works of art."

"You'll learn. Your soup is a winner. Such skills are essential. Food nourishes one's body, the eye feeds one's soul. Practise what I've shown you. When I return you'll be making orange roses as well as I do." He stroked her thigh.

Emma considered thigh-stroking to be a serious move in Canada. What did it mean in Bahrain? She moved closer.

"I must go," he announced, "to get my precious soup." He leapt up and returned to the kitchen. She followed and poured the soup into a plastic container.

"Our meeting was magical," she said, snapping a cover on the soup. "Your gifts...our conversation...overwhelmed me."

"That's because you've never been properly courted," he explained. "Western men!"

He put down the soup carton and kissed her. When she opened her eyes he swivelled around, opened the door, and strode away. From the elevator he called, "I'll phone you tomorrow."

---

Although she was so aroused after he left that she took a cold shower, the walk and soup-making had tired her, so she slept well.

She awoke feeling cosy and was eating porridge when Salim called her from the airport. "I'll return to you at winter's end and spring's beginning," he promised. "Until then, practise peeling oranges, and become accustomed to your new clothes. In order that you may observe *hijab*, I'm sending you our national costume and an *abaya* by courier. Here's Sarif — he says that you make the best soup he's ever tasted, and he's composing some music just for you."

"But what about us?"

"I will return in March, my love, as it was written."

---

Emma floats on her silky rug in the sandalwood scented room. Tenors wind down. Luciano concludes. *...Que nul ne dorme! Que nul ne dorme!...trembler d'amour et d'esperance!...* She is relieved. She won't waste any more time worrying about making pasta for Luciano.

She stretches before standing up. Then she shakes her hands, her feet; blows out the incense stick, and takes a sip of water.

She changes into her new blouse and harem pants, strokes kohl around her eyes, and admires its effect with her new *abaya*.

In the kitchen she eats pita scooped in hummus dotted with pomegranate seeds before carving an orange into a rose. She eats it segment by segment; petal by petal.

---

She saunters into the living room and puts on Sarif's CD. At first she moves sinuously, attunes herself to music so important in her new life. As the tempo accelerates she whirls and spins with such frenzy that she nearly upsets her bouquet.

When the music ceases, she falters and flings herself down on the sofa to catch her breath. She sighs, and, seeing her flowers, gets up to mist the buds again. If they don't bloom she will not grieve. Salim will bring fresh ones when he returns for her.

In March. At winter's end and spring's beginning.

# Union Station

*T*he woman dashes into the concourse and squints across the room at the GO TRAIN sign.

| 10:43 | MILTON | TRACK 2 |
|-------|--------|---------|
| 11:45 | AJAX | PLEASE WAIT HERE |
| 11:48 | OAKVILLE | PLEASE WAIT HERE |

She glances at her watch, whisks a senior's Go pass from a purple straw bag swinging from her shoulder, mouths a word that looks like 'damn,' sighs: strides up to a young man attending a cappuccino stall. He is dark, olive-skinned: absorbed in talk with three other men. They smile and gesticulate as they speak.

She moves towards them. They ignore her.

This woman is short and broad-shouldered; her expression animated, gestures quick. Her cheeks are flushed and her hazel eyes shine. A fuchsia batik kaftan floats around tanned ankles: purple sandals hug bare feet. Sun or swimming has lightened her hair ends and left the roots brown. On one side is a white streak. These blonde, brown and white patches give her hair a Calico Cat effect.

The woman beams at the cappuccino stall men and lingers near them. They ignore her. She frowns, thrusts her chin forward and marches past them to the next stall. There, a plump redhaired girl wiping the counter looks up, smiles, and speaks. The woman leans on the counter, chats, settles in. A man behind her exploring racks of muffins and pastries pushes past her to order. When the redhead turns to assist him, the woman waits. Finally she stalks toward a newsstand to look at magazines. She fingers one: returns it. When an old man steps forward to serve her, she shakes her head and turns away.

From the concourse centre she surveys rows of seats.

At one, an old greyhaired lady in a floral print house dress slumps behind a laden bundle-buggy; at another, three youths wearing York sweatshirts and shorts unload their backpacks; at a third, two suited businessmen lurk behind copies of *The Financial Post*.

The woman paces back and forth before sitting down in the emptiest section beside a jean-clad girl intently knitting. She bends across to examine the girl's work, chatting and smiling. The knitter nods, frowns: counts, sliding her finger along the needle.

The woman sits erect, re-checks timetable, watch, coffee stands. She rises: strides past the cappuccino stall, stops again at the next counter, speaks. The redhead lifts various-sized styrofoam cups. The woman chooses while engaging the girl in conversation. The redhead pours a medium cup of Colombian. The woman selects a cello-wrapped Rice Krispy square, opens her bag and pays. She takes cup, napkins, and change from the attendant, settling in at the counter until two teenagers push ahead of her to order. The teenagers dawdle. The woman picks her way to a service centre where she adds milk to her coffee. She sips some before replacing the lid, frowning from the difficulty of carrying her purchases. She beams at the knitter after she finally settles down. The knitter resumes counting.

A napkin slides off the woman's lap. She shrugs: places her coffee on an empty seat. She unwraps the Krispy square and bites into it: drops its crumpled wrapping beside her cup. After eating, she clutches her coffee and gulps it down. When finished, she stuffs cello wrap into the cup and tosses it into a nearby garbage bin.

She heads again to the newsstand: hesitates, swivels back and returns to her place. She watches people enter and leave as they cross the room from street entrance to subway: from subway to street. Sometimes she turns to the knitter, sometimes she gets up to stand beside the bundle-buggy lady who, head down, munches a sandwich. She approaches the York students. They smile and exchange hellos. When she continues talking they become busy with their packs and books. She leaves them. When she sits down again, she closes her eyes. She opens them later to check the timetable, and she lunges forward — surprised, mouth and eyes open. She calls, "Hey Bob! BOB!"

A tall, whitehaired man slouches through an entrance. He halts but does not turn. He wears a grey tweed jacket, grey slacks, white shirt, blue-and-grey striped tie. His polished black shoes are leather with heavy crepe soles. He is lean: the jacket and slacks hang loosely as if he has lost weight. A thatch of white hair combed forward to hide baldness gives the effect of a wig. He is tall, strongboned. His large brown eyes are commanding. But his nose is short, his chin small.

His entrance attracts the attention of two young women

commuters in sundresses. They watch him proceed across the room.

The woman rises, shouts, "Bob!" He halts, sighs, turns slowly. As she rushes forward he smiles, ambling to meet her. He bends to embrace her: they kiss each other's lips. He looks toward the exit, at his watch, before putting his arm around her. She leads him to the seats, slows her pace to his. The couple sit beside the knitter and talk. The knitter stops counting and knits.

The woman's voice is loud, her speech rapid. She waves her hands, opens her arms, leans towards the man. He closes his arms tightly across his waist and clutches his hands. He huddles in his seat except for moments when he turns to her, startled. Then he lifts one hand to stroke his chin as if it were a beard. Sometimes he frowns and confronts her. Mostly he hunches in his seat, his face a mask.

The woman laughs, telling his something. He smiles and winds his watch when he speaks. Her lips curl when she snarls a reply. They chuckle; and whispering, lean back together.

The man attempts to stand but falls back, grimacing. As he tries again, the woman reaches for his right hand with her left, helping him. Mimicking his distress she rises with him, rubs her own back with her right hand. Her face mirrors his pain. "I know. I know," she says.

They stand: her face lights up. She opens her mouth to speak: hesitates, closes her lips.

The man bends down, hugs her, kisses her, murmurs. Then, shoulders slumped and head down, he slouches toward the exit.

The woman skips after him but halts when he does not turn.

She stands still: watches him cross the floor, slide through the turnstile.

Once through, he looks back. They wave and exchange smiles.

When he is out of sight the woman paces the concourse until the notice board flashes—OAKVILLE TRACK 3B.

She darts to the exit waving her senior's pass and runs downstairs to catch the train.

# Osfa and The Canadian Mosaic

Jan, Wendy, Betty Ann, and I, all met when we were students at the Ontario College of Education. After graduation, we landed jobs in Toronto and rented a house in the Beaches. We'd been together four years before we met Bob MacIntosh, whom we named Mr. One-Size-Fits-All.

Our group was so close we developed a private language. Like, we called *The Globe and Mail*, 'white sliced bread.' Outsiders couldn't keep up — which was fun. Our in-group lingo.

We respected Mr. One-Size, so called him 'Osfa' publicly to protect his identity, but cracked up when outsiders thought 'Osfa' was a foreigner.

'Is this Osfa fellow a Baltic person?' or, 'Is Osfa a Scandinavian variation of Oscar?' We'd answer 'yes,' trying to keep straightfaced.

We named him Mr. One-Size-Fits-All because one after the other of us found him to be a perfect filler between real love affairs.

We hung out at Future Bakeries looking for fun and new faces. As one Futures after another got trendy, we moved west. It gets boring with the same old crowd, and moving was prudent because sometimes one of us wore out a welcome by drinking too much, or flirting too obviously. We all loved wine and guys. Usually we ended up at Futures on Bloor West near High Park, but mostly we danced at ethnic bars. College street for Spanish, Parkdale for eastern European, the Danforth for Greek.

We taught at Jonathan Swift Community College. Jan, Betty Ann, and I taught ESL to immigrants; Wendy taught College English. The ESL course was mostly oral, so there were not a lot of papers to mark. Wendy had it harder, with written assignments to prepare, which made her a drag because she complained when we played tapes and danced around the house while she graded papers.

Because of our work it was easy to understand why outsiders assumed 'Osfa' was an immigrant. Our boyfriends always were. Ex-students, brothers of students: guys from Yugo-Slavia, Macedonia, and especially Guatemala and other Spanish-speaking countries. Latins were our favourites.

I believe the attraction of such men resulted from our 'old Canadian' backgrounds. We were third generation mixtures from the British Isles. Except for Wendy, who was born in England and never let us forget it, lah-de-da. We shared a commitment to the Canadian Mosaic, an idea drilled into us in high school where we learned to be proud of 'unity in diversity,' a policy making us feel superior to Americans with their watered-down, 'Melting Pot' model. We embraced multiculturalism, because when it came to romance, imaginative women like us yearned for something different from the jocks we'd grown up with, and our passion for ethnic dancing gave immigrant men the advantage. Folk-dancing was an interest that began in dance class at OCE. As a Phys Ed option, it beat grass hockey.

Poor Mr. One-Size-Fits-All was Canadian, from Kirkland Lake or Sudbury — up North, anyway. We met him playing chess at Futures. He taught math or something at the University of Toronto. I suppose you could say he was good-looking. He was tall, well-built, sandy-haired, and into sports. He played baseball and hockey with some guys who hung out at Futures for post-game beer and carbohydrates. Canadians. Some nights we'd watch them play if there was nothing else to do.

The jocks were nice enough. They bought us pitchers of draft and tried to come on to us, but we kept it platonic. 'Platonic' is easy with Canadians.

Our group was attracted to the same type: dark, foreign, brooding men with incredible pasts, no money, and limited English. All four of us were fair, various shades of blonde. Except for Wendy, a redhead. Big deal. I guess dark men found us attractive because our looks contrasted with theirs.

Declarations of love sound so magical in foreign languages. Our love affairs were intense: the topic of endless telephone conversations and inter-collegiate E-mail.

Even when involved in serious affairs, we indulged in heavy flirtations with waiters at ethnic bars where we drank and danced up a storm. We were so obviously foreign to them that they fussed over us: impressed by our ability to dance their dances. They sneaked us free drinks which was only fair because we drew a lot of customers who either danced with us or enjoyed watching us.

Some of these waiters had been professionals in their own countries — lawyers, teachers — now working in Toronto at whatever jobs they found until they improved their English, qualified for citizenship, and moved on to better jobs. Admirable, but rather a pity. We liked them right off the boat, just the way they were when they arrived. Foreign waiters are so cute.

Before I met Osfa I was living with Viktor, a Bulgarian. Until the night his wife tracked him down at our place, and through an interpreter over long distance telephone, screamed at me for 'stealing my husband!' A wife of whose existence I was unaware. Right after Viktor grabbed the phone I was heading for the bathroom where I swallowed a bottle of Ativan pills.

The Ativan — pumped out at East General after Viktor phoned the ambulance — did not do the trick. Wendy told the college I had flu. I was back at work in a week.

That was another nice thing about foreign men. Suicide attempts during or near the end of a romance they regarded as appropriate behaviour — the stuff of passion —not leftovers from early childhood trauma to discuss with a shrink. Viktor took the Ativan episode in his stride: I forgave him for withholding information about his wife.

I really loved Viktor, who worked in a warehouse as a shipper-receiver for a temp agency. I loved how tough and rough he looked setting out for work early in the morning in overalls and workboots. I was knocked for a loop when he disappeared. I assumed he'd returned to the wife in Bulgaria until a student told me that he'd gone to work in a mine near Whitehorse. So much for upward mobility.

My housemates worried about me. They'd over-reacted to the Ativan overdose and kept dragging me out to old haunts. Everywhere except to The Bulgarian Palace where I'd danced and drank with Viktor.

That was how I happened to meet Bob—a.k.a Osfa. They

took me to Futures to play chess. I was good at chess, and because I had to concentrate, it took my mind off Viktor.

Osfa was hanging around drinking with some ballplayers and joined a group of people watching me. An audience never put me off. After I won, clobbering an old Russian man who was a champ of sorts, Osfa challenged me to a game. He won. I must have been tired by then. Although Osfa was an expert player.

What drew Osfa into our fold was a brotherly quality which inspired trust. After he bought me a cognac, I told him my whole sordid tale. When my friends saw me in safe hands, they took off to go dancing.

Bob — I called him Bob at first — walked me all the way to the Chester subway and finally home. He hated cars — something I knew our group would approve of. We were environmentalists, although our immigrant lovers always bought cars as soon as they found work. Something to prove their success in the New World, I guess.

Bob telephoned the very next day and invited me to dinner. A date. I'd forgotten about dates. Usually we hit ethnic spots Friday and Saturday nights. When an immigrant guy danced with me, and there was that spark, a serious relationship followed.

In the bleak, post-Viktor time, Bob was my prize, my shoulder, my date. We went out for dinner, to films, to plays; we walked, we talked. I told him all about myself — my rotten mother, my over-achieving brother, my ne'er-do-well father. Bob was a great listener.

My friends envied my dates with Bob, but there wasn't that competitive aspect, evident when two of us had a crush on the same guy. Bob just wasn't in the running, so at first we named him 'old faithful,' because he always took along whichever one of my housemates was at loose ends. There was never that spark there, between us, and I'd hate to have dumped him when I met someone I was attracted to.

So I was relieved when Betty Ann was abandoned by her Chilean lover, Jaime, returning to his dying mother in Santiago. By then I'd met Yuri, one night out dancing.

I told Bob all about Betty Ann's despair, and suggested he help her through it, the way he had with me. I softened the blow to his ego by saying I was afraid to grow too dependent on him, after what I'd been through with Viktor. Honestly, he couldn't have been more understanding. I expected a scene, but all he said was, "I'd be happy to see Betty Ann." I guess it's just Canadian coolness. A relief, but bland, bland.

Soon Bob was dating Betty Ann and hearing her story. If I hadn't already gotten steamy with Yuri, I'd have envied her. Restaurants, social events. Dates.

Betty Ann was enthusiastic. "Bob's so understanding! What a listener!"

When Wendy overheard Betty Ann raving about what they'd eaten at Fiasco's after a film at the Revue, she piped up, 'Good old One-Size-Fits All!' We roared. Of course the name stuck and that was how we always referred to him among ourselves.

This name grew more appropriate when Jan discovered that her Greek boyfriend, Takis, was engaged to a Greek girl. One of those old world arrangements. Takis assured her he did not love this other woman, but that his father had a heart condition and would probably die if his son didn't go through with the engagement. We avoided the Danforth because there was a big celebration coming up between the families and we didn't want to make things worse for poor Jan by stumbling into that scene.

Betty Ann asked lots of questions about this Greek arrangement. We discovered why when she announced, "It's Jan's turn to spend some time with Osfa. I didn't want to upset you, but when Jaime left for Chile I applied for work in Saudi Arabia. After what I went through with him, and what Nancy went through with Viktor, I decided that I was going to be the romantic foreigner. My job in Ryad allows for paid vacations which I plan to spend in Paris, Rome, Madrid —picking up the cutest men I see and leaving them behind. So it would be a good idea to explain to Osfa about Jan. He'll be a brick. He's taken to my move well — understood and offered to help. You know. Packing, shipping. The messy stuff."

"He didn't even try to talk you out of it?" I asked.

"No. Was his usual understanding self. Just listened. I'm glad Jan will be here to fill the gap. The two can get close when he comes to help me pack."

It went as we hoped. Bob asked Jan out the night after Betty Ann left. He took her to see *Phantom of the Opera*, which gave her the opportunity to cry on his shoulder and be comforted, before launching into her saga of Takis and his Greek import.

"Osfa is a prince,' Jan said. 'I didn't know there were guys like that. So interested in my problems. He's just what I need now."

Meanwhile, out in Saudi Arabia, Betty Ann was running up phone bills. She was homesick. She missed us. We were afraid she'd use up her money phoning and have none left for romantic travel. So we were excited when she spoke of a trip to Ankara. Turks! Wild dancing! We awaited news of foreign affairs.

You could have blown us over with a feather when she

telephoned several weeks later and told us that while in Ankara she'd met a Canadian engineer. From Burlington! Worse still, they were engaged and returning to Toronto for the wedding next spring.

I was still happy with Yuri; Jan still dated Osfa. Either Osfa didn't let on, or was ignoring Jan eyeing a guy she met at Tapas. Not that Fernando, who was from the Azores, was picking up her cues. Jan still needed Osfa.

We all needed him. It gave us security to know that if a relationship broke up or didn't work out, Osfa would be there; with his 'dates,' his shoulder, his desire to listen, to empathize. I wondered if he might be gay, putting up with us the way he did without hitting on us. Really weird behaviour. He must have found us interesting or he wouldn't have bothered. I guess we seemed exciting to him, coming as he did from the northern boonies.

We were relieved and annoyed when he told us he was going home for Christmas. 'Home' turned out to be some-place called Haileybury. We soon found our own name for this village. Hellburg. We were annoyed because except for the ball team and his job, we couldn't imagine him with any life without us. But we were relieved because we planned to throw an international Christmas party for our boyfriends. Osfa would not have fit in because Jan felt it would be an ideal event to which she could invite Fernando. Not too obvious a ploy, but a chance to get to know him.

The party was not a success. Poor Jan. Fernando was a lush, and not a pleasant one. He became belligerent; made provocative political comments to Yuri and Carlos, threw up, and spoiled everything. We comforted Jan by assuring her that when Osfa returned, we would have a better party at New Year's.

When Osfa phoned from Hellburg, fortunately I answered.

"Hi Nance," he said. "Is Jan around?"

"She's out now. Any message?"

"Yes," he said. "I know you were planning something for New Year's, but I won't be back by then. I'm staying on up here with my folks."

"Really?" I asked. "What can you do away up there?"

He explained, "My dad is a prof at the mines school. Every New Year's there's a bash. It's a family obligation. I've a date with a close family friend."

"Sounds like a blast, Bob," I said. "I'll explain to Jan."

"Jan will be okay," he assured me. "I'll call again. In the meantime, have fun. I've known your gang long enough to know that you always do."

When I relayed this message to the others, we all hooted, wondering what kind of dancing they did up in Hellburg, outside of the barns. And 'obligation?' That word was not in our vocabulary. We tried to imagine the date his 'folks' talked him into. The village wallflower. That would be like our Osfa, helping out a dateless damsel. But he was *our* Osfa. We resented him rescuing damsels outside our group.

We did make hay during his absence. Jan set her sights on a Mexican, a Ryerson student who spoke English. This was a relief, because during our encounters, except for essential pillow talk, we never learned our lovers' languages. Greek and the Eastern block were excusable because of the crazy alphabets. What mattered to us was not language, but dancing and sex.

However, Spanish is a practical language. Mexican students have families we might even be invited to visit.

"Nance, I'm sick of refugees," Jan explained.

"You've got a point," I agreed.

Osfa telephoned again.

"Hi, Nance. Are you on permanent phone duty?"

"No, Bob," I snapped. "I'm waiting for a call from Yuri."

"No problem. Actually, that's cool. You know your way around. I want to find the best Turkish night club in Toronto. I'm bringing back a guest — my New Year's date, and I want to show her some exotic spots."

His announcement threw us. Had the guy lost it? We giggled again at the thought of some northern ingenue, wide-eyed at a Turkish restaurant. Even I didn't know any, but Yuri, to my surprise, said he did.

"Eastern dancing," he said. "The Tent of Omar. Very nice. Very sexy!"

That must have been before we met, because he'd never taken me there. And worse, it was to-hell-and-gone in Mississauga. The food and dance, Yuri assured us, was 'Very nice. Very nice like in Turkey.' Yuri had worked on Russian merchant ships and travelled everywhere, so we knew we could count on him.

The big shock came when Osfa returned. This woman, Berna, that he had in tow, was not only from Turkey and an engineer — a mining engineer — but drove a puce-coloured Saab hatchback. Osfa said Saabs were practical for northern roads during long rough winters, but the damned gas-guzzler looked like a mobile eggplant to me.

Berna was gorgeous. Too gorgeous. Great hair, great dusky skin, great figure. Poor Osfa would need our support when she returned to some guy back in Turkey.

But no. This Berna person was staying on in Hellburg. She was a professor at something called the International School of Mines, apparently attended by people from all over the world. No wonder Osfa understood the foreign men we went out with.

"Why, Wendy," I asked, "why did Osfa never tell us about himself? About Hellburg, about this big mining school where his father was a professor?"

"Because," she answered, "he was listening to us. We never asked him anything. We were always telling him all about our problems."

Saturday night we piled into Berna's Saab. I admit she was a good sport, although she flirted a bit too much with Yuri and Carlos. I thought Turkish women were supposed to be subjected and oppressed.

Poor Osfa. How must he feel about her behaviour? It was hard to tell, because he hadn't stopped smiling since he got back. Talk about denial!

Flirting is one thing. Belly-dancing is another. There were Jan, Wendy and I, sitting beside our poor guys with their tongues hanging out while Berna was bumping and grinding. The band loved it, the crowd clapped and stamped their feet.

The only good part of the evening was when some gorgeous Turkish hunks came to our table, sat down and bought us drinks. When Berna got back they started jabbering in Turkish, although one guy asked if we came here often, and seeing that Wendy was dateless, asked for her number.

I think the least Osfa could have done was to have told us about himself. All along we felt we were doing him a favour by providing him with our company, and he kept us in the dark. What hurt most was that he told us nothing about his important plans.

He'd given Berna a diamond engagement ring for Christmas. Big enough for a whole mining company. His engagement could not have happened overnight. Osfa must have known Berna all along. No wonder he'd had a hands-off policy with us — deceitful behaviour that made us doubt our attractiveness at a time when we had just been rejected. His lack of regard was shocking, considering the extent to which we shared with him our innermost thoughts and all the intimate details of our loves.

Because Betty Ann is getting married she won't be so hurt by Osfa's defection. Jan is still going strong with her Mexican, and Wendy is dating one of the Turkish students and learning to belly dance.

I can't be bothered travelling out to Mississauga when I know I'm one of the best dancers of salsa and merengue in Toronto. So I stick to Spanish bars downtown where I'm appreciated, and where waiters are generous with the wine.

Recently I enrolled in a Russian language class at the college. Yuri is pleased, even though it means we can't make it out to the Turkish place. Saturday is the only night we are both free to have him help me with my Russian. That bloody Cyrillic alphabet is the pits.

Osfa recently redeemed himself. Last week he hit us with wonderful news. We are invited to his book launch! The book must be about political science. I just assumed he taught math because of his great chess game. His publishers must have made a mistake. The announcement states that he is 'a professor of English,' and although the book title is *Canadian Mosaic*, the blurb describes it as a 'collection of short fiction.'

He valued us enough to include us in his triumph. Sitting through a reading on immigration policy will be a drag, but he is *our* Osfa, our dear, dear friend. And of course, there'll be free wine.

# Guilt Trips

For Jeremy

*A*fter the eighth race Patrick and I leave, dashing through a downpour of rain to catch the bus. I sit up in front close to the driver. I like it up here, because the passengers getting on are always excited, eager to bare their souls to someone, whatever their fates have been, and I'm sneaky enough to be curious. It's almost as if the fare box is like a collection box beside the confessional.

The sign on the bus reads — RACES — and after looking around I decide that this sign refers to the ethnicity of the passengers. Opposite me two old Chinese women count wins and losses, their voices clicking like abacus beads. A smiling Jamaican leaps aboard and announces to the driver, "Mon, I sure hot today! I win every goddamn race!" At least, I assume he's Jamaican because his T-shirt reads GENJA UNIVERSITY.

A young East Indian couple are entwined on a seat up the aisle. They are beautiful, they are winners, and their winning has nothing to do with Woodbine. The day is young. I smile, sensing a heavy bet ahead.

At the very back sits my husband Patrick. I watch him out of the corner of my eye light his Tuero and tilt back his head. He appears smug — not just the way cigar smokers always seem to do — but because he'd won enough in the third race to take us out to dinner. I feel omnipotent as I watch him close his eyes, draw on the cigar, then slowly exhale, for I am seeing his Shadow, the gambling man that hides within the respectable computer consultant.

The driver counts passengers, then looks at his watch. "They're late," he tells us upfronters. "The last race should be over by now."

I'm about to examine Patrick's Shadow again when a middle-aged man wearing a Burberry climbs on. He thrusts two dollars through the fare-box, looks around, then plunks down beside me.

I'm annoyed by his presence because I need distance from people after all the excitement at the clubhouse. So does Patrick, which is why he sits at the back and smokes cigars. At least that's what he tells me, when I complain about the cigar smoke.

Judging from this newcomer's animated entrance, he will want to talk. I appraise him carefully. He's not bad-looking, but not memorable. Blah-brown hair, blah-complexion, blah-eyes. He's just a bland, no-name generic Caucasian. He is carrying an umbrella and wearing rubbers — both signs, in my book, of a mother's boy, a careful man, a bachelor.

"I thought I might as well take this bus," he tells me, as if we're old friends or I care what he does or something. "Although I've another bet on in the ninth. When I won a bundle on the eighth I thought there was no point in hanging around in this weather."

"Boy did I win! A lot. Bet to place, but the man made an

error and punched me to win. So I thought, what the heck, it's the eighth race. So I bet over again to place. Two bets!" He slaps his thigh.

He must be loaded. The odds had been twelve to one on the winning horse, a gorgeous roan filly. I'd wanted to bet on her because I love roans, and because I feel it's politically correct to bet on fillies. I'd watched her coming onto the field — edgy, sharp, prancing to her post. A winner. I begged Patrick, pushing the racing form at him and pointing out her Irish sire of strong Kildare stock. But Patrick, the educated handicapper, said no, the numbers weren't right, so he wouldn't let me place a bet. I was miffed, because I felt that I was beginning to perceive a winner from the look of the horses and how they moved, not from racing form stats and computer printouts. But there was no arguing with Patrick, because by then he had already won enough to take me out to our favourite Yugoslavian restaurant. "No point in you taking a risk, a beginner betting a long shot," he'd told me.

Obviously I had begun to enjoy the track which my upbringing had made me feel was evil. 'Filthy lucre,' 'no sweat of the brow.' But after I met Patrick and he took me to Woodbine I was hooked. From the very beginning I loved the people and their excitement, traditions like the Queen's Plate, the thrill of betting. And I especially loved the Jockey Club hot roast beef sandwiches. They don't taste that good anywhere else in Toronto.

Most of all, I enjoy Patrick's rationalizations for betting. He's so creative. He is no mere gambler. Oh, no. He always tells me before and after these excursions that he goes to the track to explore Jung's theories of synchronicity, to exercise the right side of his brain, to test laws of probability, or to try out a new computer system. He even claimed that he bets to prove he is not hooked on gambling. He has other reasons, many of them so elaborate and scientific that I can't understand them. Although I like the one about track attendance being our patriotic duty, because Northern Dancer was the greatest Canadian in history.

I try to sneak another look at him when the guy beside me leans over. "The track is healthy," the man says. "It's good for me; I need to get out in the fresh air."

I turn to look at him. I'm interested, because his statement has all the signs of another guilt-ridden, middle-class professional rationalizing his love of gambling.

"Don't you agree?" he persists. I don't respond right away, because I know what he wants. He wants my permission.

Finally I bite. "Yes, I do. I also see the track as entertainment, like a play." I know this line by heart. One of Patrick's favourites. I quote, " 'Some people think nothing of going out and spending a lot more on dinner and a show than you probably do at the track.' "

"Absolutely!" the guy beams. "That's exactly how I look at it! And I get the fresh air, and on good days, the sun." He pauses, then explains, "You see, I don't get out much."

I'm curious. Why does he have to stay indoors? He's baiting me to ask. I know the cues. But I won't bite, although I do wonder about this man's preoccupation with health and his desperate need to relate to total strangers. What's with him, anyway? I wait.

"Mind you, I'm not a fanatic," he says. "If you want fanatics, now just take your runners. Why, I've a man, high up in the government, runs ten miles a day. I don't know when he finds time for his wife," he chuckles.

I am wearing a track suit and brand new Nikes. Is he

retaliating because I didn't seem interested in his need for fresh air? Have I hurt him, played into his guilt thing about health? No wonder, with all those fitness ads everywhere these days. He probably thinks he should be out playing golf. But who is this bureaucrat 'high up in the government?' And what did he mean, 'I've got a man?' What is their relationship? Is he this man's doctor, dentist, lawyer? He is his doctor, I decide. He's definitely a doctor. Now my curiosity gets the better of me. Maybe a confession from me would elicit more information from him.

"I run myself," I volunteer. "Nothing like ten miles a day though." I worry. Have I said the wrong thing? Will I make him feel even guiltier?

"Where do you run?"

"Along the Lakeshore." He will probably wonder if I live in High Park or Parkdale, but he's too polite to ask. There's such a big difference, socio-economically. I'm from lowdown Parkdale, which is harness-racing territory, but High Park's more of a thoroughbred community.

He must have guessed High Park, for he leans against me presumptuously and says, "I'm going to strip a dry sink tomorrow. Picked it up in Nova Scotia last summer. Was there on tour with my church group."

His shoulder's pressure makes me uneasy and I edge away, but the church group reference reassures me.

"I've never been to Nova Scotia," I answer, "but I do have a dry sink. From Quebec." I don't add that tomorrow I'll be stripping eighty years of history and about forty coats of paint from my front door. He might think I was moving too fast, mentioning my antiques, trying to show how much we had in common.

"See that house there?" He turns around and points over

my shoulder. I crane my neck. "That's the old Rothwell place. Lovely home. I've been all through it. When the Rothwells owned it. You know the Rothwells, of course."

I don't, but he doesn't give me time to answer.

"A fine old building," he enthuses. "Don't know who lives there now. I bought six oak chairs when they sold it. Couldn't get them for love nor money today. Not chairs like those."

"I only knew the Rothwells slightly, of course," he continues. "My sister knew them better. Sang in the church choir with Margaret Rothwell. They became great friends. She was an alto. My sister, that is. Margaret is a soprano, I believe."

La-de-dah. Obviously *everyone* has heard of these Rothwells. They probably own thoroughbreds.

Suddenly he turns to me and asks, "Do you sing?"

"Yes."

"Thought so. Soprano?"

"Yes."

"Any choral work?"

"Yes."

"United Church?"

"Yes."

Dear God, I'm being screened! For a duet?

Now I'm sorry my curiosity about this total stranger led me to ignore the existence of Patrick puffing away and polluting the air at the back. But if I mention a husband now, all of a sudden, it would be too obvious, too insulting.

"I don't think I'll go out to dinner," the guy muses. "Too wet, don't you think?"

Oh, so he might have asked me out. What's wrong with me, besides my track suit? Is he just too shy, or would he have invited me if I were an alto? What's he got against sopranos anyway? Margaret was good enough for his sister. "I put a kidney to marinate," he informs me. "Might as well eat that. Do you like kidney?"

"Yes."

But not that one. I decided several miles ago that this man is a doctor, which makes everything he's told me sound sinister. I imagine seeing a human kidney soaking in a basin in his kitchen. I edge away. "My Lord," he goes on. "It's a huge kidney." He laughs. Then, suddenly serious, he adds, "Don't know if I really like them that large. But it'll be good."

He leans towards me and adds confidentially, "You see, I know all the vets." There he goes trying to impress me again, but instead, I'm scared.

Why does he know all the vets? Doctors and vets go to different schools. And where does the runner fit in? Oh dear. Runners have large hearts. I've read that. I can just see him lurking behind bushes, camouflaged by surgeon's greens, scalpel in hand, waiting for some poor innocent jogger...

"No," he continues, "I won't go out tonight just because it's Saturday, and I've made a killing. I'll stay home and have my kidney."

*Killing.* I panic and look desperately for Patrick. He's staring out the window. I can't move away from the man now, that would increase his suspicions. I should have taken a self-defense course at the Y. I should carry mace in my purse.

In an attempt to calm myself I focus on the Indian couple, who are disentwining. The girl turns away from the young man, cool. I approve of her indifference, because I'm glad there a few nice girls left. I'm sure her boyfriend understands. He's probably been strictly brought up. Both of them have. "I'll serve it with broccoli and baked potatoes," the doctor says. "And a salad. You like broccoli, of course."

He expects me for dinner! I can just imagine him showing off the pine antiques in the living room, then leading me to his white, sterile kitchen. He'll pull out a chair for me, bring a kidney from the counter and place it over a Bunsen burner on the table. Then he'd sharpen his knife and smile.

He moves closer; and terrified, I force my mind from dinner at his place, and rivet my attention on the Chinese women. While they talk, I follow their eyes to the race programmes they are comparing. Chinese characters line the margins. I crane my neck to see, as if I were in the habit of reading Cantonese upside down.

He persists. "Yes, it's really too wet to go out to dinner. What do you think?"

Well, at least he respects my opinion. "It depends," I say. But now I know why he's a bachelor. He's a cheapskate doctor. Gouges medical insurance, swipes kidneys from hospital incinerators. Preys on runners.

We near Islington and the Indian girl asks to be let off. Her friend stays. They exchange no parting kisses, no words.

Why? Did my stares make this young woman feel guilty? Does her mother disapprove? Is it a cultural thing? Was this a forbidden date? If so, why didn't they head for a park instead of wasting time at the track?

We are reaching High Park right now. When I see the flowering-cherry trees that line the roadside, their beauty brings me back to earth. We're nearly home. I sigh with relief. Now it's safe to be friendly.

"Aren't those trees lovely?" I ask the man.

"Gorgeous. What are they? Plum"?

"No. Flowering-cherry trees. A gift from the Japanese government to the city of Toronto." I learned this from Patrick on the way out, and I'm pleased to pass the information along. Patrick always gives me a great conducted tour on the way to the track — anything to keep me from nagging at him about betting.

The man slaps his thigh and smiles. I figure that he shares my enthusiasm for the cherry trees, and the generosity of the Japanese. Our encounter will end happily after all. It'll be okay. When we part, I'll even wish him luck on the ninth.

"Can you beat that!" he says, pointing to his pant cuff. "I always win when the cuff is turned up! I just noticed it." He's chortling crazily, but pauses to add, "and, of course, five dollar bills are unlucky. I have to change them all before I go near Woodbine."

"Oh? Really?"

"Another thing is unlucky — if someone wishes me luck." He tells me, just as we pull into Sunnyside.

So much for my good intentions.

"Nice chatting with you," I say. "Have a pleasant week."

I hurry to the centre exit and stand by Patrick. The bus slows down and the Chinese women scurry ahead. The Jamaican still grins as he strolls down the street to the car-stop. I clutch Patrick and watch the crazy doctor run across the street against the red light. Brakes screech. The East Indian walks off in the opposite direction.

———

We stroll up Roncesvalles to the restaurant, find a table and sit down. The waitress brings menus.

"No need for these," says Patrick, handing them back. "A Wooden Platter for two and a bottle of Plavac." I touch his extended hand. "No, no, Patrick! I want the white wine. And just a salad please."

"But you've been screaming for a Wooden Platter, and we always drink red!"

"I know, I know, Patrick. But I changed my mind. I couldn't face all that meat. And red wine looks so bloody!"

The waitress waits; shrugs, then drops the menus on the table and stalks off.

"All I want is a Greek salad," I tell Patrick.

"I'll never understand you! I only bet because I promised you a Wooden Platter if we won, and now you don't even want it. What's got into you this time?" He picks up a menu and says, "Well, if you want white wine, I guess I might as well go with the fish."

The waitress returns to take our order, then brings a bottle of Blue Nun for Patrick to taste. When she's gone, I lean across the table.

He puts down his glass. "What is it? Now what's wrong?"

"Patrick, there's something I've got to find out." I really want to ask him who the Rothwells are, and why doctors who go to the track might know veterinarians, but I'll just have to worry about those problems. I've decided to be more assertive.

"Patrick," I ask, "about that roan filly? How much would I have won, and how come all the stats were against her?"

Gosh, I'm getting good at this, too, I think, watching Patrick frown and top our glasses while he struggles to dream up a reply.

# The Kettle Valley Celebrations

'Along the Kettle Valley Line.'

'The little Japanese dancers.'

'May Queen Mary Jeffers and her retinue.'

'The Doukabor choir.'

# The Golden Jubilee: 1947

*I* hate this train because it takes too darned long and these green plush seats are so old they stink. Their coal smell makes me sick to my stomach.

The uniformed newsie pushes into the day coach and calls, "Sandwiches! Soft drinks!" Gosh, I'm hungry. The trip is nearly over, but Mom said I should eat something so I wouldn't get trainsick.

"Just ginger ale, please," I say. That should be enough to settle my stomach. I'm trying to save money, and besides, there's not much choice in the day coach. Cheese or ham sandwiches, milk or pop. I hand the newsie a dollar. He opens the bottle, sticks in a straw, gives me back my change and swerves down the aisle while the train rolls along. I keep thinking of the diner at the back, where Pullman car passengers get nice hot meals, and where they have linen-covered tables set with real silver.

I'm lucky, in a way, to even be in the day coach. I get a pass that lets me ride on the CPR free, any time I need to, because Dad worked on the railway. He was a conductor. He didn't work on passenger trains, just freight trains. I'm still embarrassed, telling people that about Dad, because Kettle Valley is a railroad town, and there's a whole set of snobbery to do with the different kinds of work men do. Passenger trains are considered classier than freight, and there are ideas of how important different jobs are. Brakeman at the bottom, then engineer, and conductor at the top. At least Dad had been a conductor. What I really hated about his work was that it kept him away from home. I used to wait to hear the train whistle blow when I was little, a signal that he was on his way back. I still miss him. Now when I first hear that whistle, I forget for a minute that he died. I guess I miss him so much because he made all the fun in our family. Mother said she gave us our brains.

I finish my ginger ale. I really love ginger ale because at home we were only allowed to have it as a special treat or when we were sick. It's the same way with oranges.

There goes the train whistle! That means we're nearing Kettle Valley. Home sweet home, yech! I wanted to stay in Vancouver where people are really sophisticated. That's where I belong. We pass Observation Mountain, the slough, some stores and houses, and finally slow down. The engine makes a funny hiss when we stop at the station. I know for sure Mom won't be there, because she doesn't meet trains or see people off. She's too emotional. I look out and see Terry, my sister Madge's boyfriend. Gosh, he looks handsome in his Mountie's uniform. There are various people at the station. I'm reminded that train arrivals are still a big event here. Some people have nothing else to look forward to, others come out of curiosity. Meeting trains was fun during the war. We'd run down after school and talk to servicemen who got off and dashed over to the hotel to pick up cases of beer. Local gossips came down to keep track of what was going on. *Why did his wife never see him off, but come to meet him?* There's nobody here today that I recognize at first. Just newcomers, *The Courier* reporter who writes up the visitors in the locals column, some kids, a couple who kiss each other, and the stationmaster Mr Jackson, who sees me, waves and yells, "Welcome home, Jenny!" After the porter helps me down, I step off and Terry rushes over to grab my suitcase and give me a hug.

"Hi there! This way, Jenny." He leads me to the RCMP car and holds the door for me to get in. I feel important being seen with him, until he says, "Your mom is knocking herself out with rehearsals. She's got you lined up for something in her big Jubilee pageant."

"Oh no, she hasn't," I announce. "I've been hired to work in the hospital. I won't have any free time for rehearsals. Besides, it's only a dumb Kettle Valley thing."

"We'll see." He grins. "Want to bet?"

----

"Uh-one two three kick! Uh-one two three glide, uh-one two three kick and cr-oss over!" Miss Dove, a newcomer to Kettle Valley, barks at us. We're practising our dance in the Jubilee's Gay Nineties item. This dumb chorus is beneath me. I wish I could have stayed in Vancouver, gone to summer school, kept on in UBC's drama club after my success playing Irina in *The Three Sisters*. The review in *The Vancouver Province* called me a gifted young actress. But I've got to work to pay next year's tuition. This pageant of Mother's is such a come-down, after Chekhov, but I can't get out of it because of what people might say.

Kettle Valley people are so narrow and small-town. I

always wanted to know what it was like, behind the mountains. Now that I've mingled with sophisticated people in a big city like Vancouver, back here I feel trapped and closed in.

'*Everyone* is taking part,' Mom insisted. 'This Jubilee pageant is the most important cultural event in Kettle Valley history. I've even got Sons of Freedom on the same program as the Orthodox Doukhobors. A first. I put up a real fight with the committee to let me include Doukhobors and Japanese because I knew it was vital to present all elements of our community. So there's no way my own daughter can back out. You absolutely have to dance in the Gay Nineties chorus. Every woman in town who can walk is in it!

'It's important to prove I am cooperating with that Miss Dove. There was bitter rivalry over which one of us would get the United Church basement for practices. I should have gotten it, being a pioneer and more involved with the church, but she insisted that the basement had the only stage suitable for dance practice. Some of the pageant officials agreed with me about dancing in the church being inappropriate, but that newcomer Miss Dove managed to acquire a following, so she got it. If you back out of her Gay Nineties dance routine, people will think I'm holding a grudge.'

I caught Mom's use of 'that' before Miss Dove, her way of showing she hates someone. Mom is a Tory, and always calls our Prime Minister 'that Mackenzie King.'

She was right about everyone participating. Two of my ancient Sunday school teachers, the Misses Dougall, were dancing. So was Joan MacDonald, the high school principal; several housewives, and the new hospital matron — my boss Barbara Sutherland, an ex-army nurse who's way over thirty. The girls — myself, and friends home from normal school or university, are dancing in the front row. After practices we giggle about the old fogies in the back. I hate 'the chorus line.' as Miss Dove calls it. For one thing, she just doesn't appeal to me. She's a plain old book-keeper with short grey hair and oxfords. What does she know about dancing? For another thing, I'm tired from working nightshift all week, jitterbugging at lake dances Saturdays and staying up late necking with Tom Morrison, a new guy from Vancouver who has a summer job in the Forestry Branch.

At first I thought Tom was a real catch because he's going back to UBC in the fall when I do, so there's a possibility of him inviting me to formals. He belongs to a fraternity, and although I disapprove of frats, they have the best dances. Really posh.

I dropped Tom right after I met Keith Thompson, the new high school teacher and our church choir accompanist. Keith is tall, shy, and comes by our house to visit and play the piano. I'm attracted to him because he's older, a musician, and from Vancouver, so naturally he's bound to be more sophisticated than home-town guys.

All frat boys are fast; Green Room actors are scary when drunk; and local boys are just like brothers. The way Terry is, because he's Madge's boyfriend.

Madge got her pick of guys during the war when the only available men in Kettle Valley were Mounties, 4F bank tellers, and visiting servicemen. She's redheaded, leggy, and a great dancer. Terry still hangs around and visits Mom, even after Madge's bank transferred her to Victoria, because he and Madge have an understanding. He comes for Sunday dinner, plays cribbage with me, and sometimes drives me to work. I used to like having him around, but now I yearn for Keith's visits.

I love singing along while Keith plays, and even, after two years away at university, of achieving new status by calling a high school teacher by his first name. In Kettle Valley first names aren't used, especially with professionals. I want Keith for my boyfriend, but it's been hard to get anywhere with him in our house, where he acts brotherly. It's the only way he could act with Mom always around. I can't stop daydreaming about him because I've been set off by hearing things from Phoebe and Beth, who have 'done it.' They brag and tell me there's nothing like it. They both did it with older men. Phoebe with an artist, Beth with her math prof. Because I lack their experience, for the first time in my life I'm a follower. I have to catch up. The sooner the better.

Dreaming of Keith, I step to Miss Dove's command. Phoebe and Beth beam like can-can dancers I've seen in pictures on French posters; the older ladies giggle.

"Perk up there, Jenny," old Dove calls, frowning at me but not missing a beat, continuing her "Uh-one two three kick! Uh-one two three glide."

---

After practice, Phoebe, Beth, and I stroll down to the drugstore for cokes and to meet the guys playing the parts of 1914 war vets. At least I have a job. Poor Phoebe and Beth have nothing to do but hang out down here in the afternoon and compare suntans or play Monopoly. No wonder they think the dumb Jubilee is such a big event that they're thrilled going to rehearsals.

Pete Smith, who was my high school boyfriend, leaps up

beside me on a stool and orders a double cherry coke, my favourite; and lemon coke for himself.

"Pete, this is too much! I'll never finish."

"You need it after dancing. I hear Dove really puts you through your paces. All we do is march on to *When Johnny Comes Marching Home*, and look solemn holding guns while they play the *Last Post*." He plays around with a straw, then says, "That bugle sound makes me sad, you know. It reminds me of Jake."

"Me too." Actually, I'm thinking of my brother Fred, and how we waited so long after he was reported missing in action, before the government told us he was taken prisoner. My other two brothers were luckier, being pilots in the Air Force. I guess they were all lucky because they came back. I still remember how I used to hear Mom cry at night, worrying; and how scared I was.

Fred was so much fun before the war. I don't know what he's really like, now. In Vancouver at least I can visit him out at Shaughnessy Military Hospital, even though I hate it in there with all those poor men. I visit Fred because he used to be my favourite brother. He has something the army doctors call combat fatigue. Sometimes he's so upset I'm told not to visit. Mostly he's okay, and we talk and play cribbage. He always wins, because in spite of the war and combat fatigue, Fred is still the smartest one in our family.

Jake Bingham was Pete's buddy all through school. He got into the army just before the war ended. Just in time to go overseas. Just in time to be killed in action.

We're all very quiet, sipping our cokes and remembering, until Jamie Hughes raises his glass. "Here's to the Jubilee!" We clink glasses, just like a real toast and say, "To the Jubilee!"

I'm relieved. Jamie has a knack for doing the right thing. We stop remembering the war.

"How about coming to the lake dance with me Saturday, Jen?" Pete asks. Ho hum. It's been his usual offer to me ever since I was first allowed to date, but he got more insistent after Tom hit town. "Sorry. I might have to work. My schedule changed." Actually, I know for sure that I'm switching to a 7-to-3 day shift just so I can attend the post-pageant dance. I will be free, Saturday, but I refuse Pete. I keep hoping that tomorrow, after dancing with Keith, he'll treat me differently. I don't flirt or anything, but I've learned that there's nothing like darkness and a slow waltz to get things going.

Pete shrugs and says, "Well, at least save me a dance tomorrow."

"Sure." I suck on the straw until it rattles in the empty glass. "Thanks. That coke was good. It'll get me through nightshift. We have to drink strong coffee to keep going. By morning I'm so sick to my stomach I can't eat."

"Sounds tough. My job's okay. Just chewing the fat with people in the store. What I've done all my life."

His dad owns the drugstore, and Pete is studying pharmacy so he can take over. We girls are embarrassed when we have to buy sanitary napkins, so always wait until we see Pete's sister May at work before we buy them. We also overhear the guys whispering about stuff Pete learns, selling certain drugstore items.

I slide off the stool. Pete gets our cokes free, so we leave. The boys go off to play baseball; I go home to change for work. Phoebe and Beth walk with me. On our way, they talk about what they're going to wear to the dance after the pageant.

"Anything will feel good after those old dresses," Phoebe says. "How could women wear them?"

"They're awful," Beth agrees. "The lacing up the back of my costume made me feel like Scarlett O'Hara! It will rip if I take a deep breath."

"I know," I agree. "But we've got to take special care of them. They belonged to Mrs Doctor Horne's and Mrs Doctor Matthews' grandmothers. Heirlooms, Mom said."

"Mrs Doctor Horne, Mrs Doctor Matthews, lah-de-dah," Beth sneers.

Phoebe adds, "Yeah. They have nothing to do with the likes of us."

"Doctors and their families can't get close to people, Phoebe. Miss Sutherland warned me about all that. Nothing I see or hear at work may be discussed outside the hospital. It's not that doctors' wives are snobby. It's just professional ethics." I feel good. I've shut them up and gotten the upper hand again.

---

At home I change into my uniform: white cotton button-down-the-front dress, stockings, white oxfords. I imagine myself looking like pictures of Miss Sutherland in her army nurse's veil and blue uniform. I keep wondering about her life when she served in Africa with the troops, and about all her romances. She must have had lots of romances because she's still pretty. And even if she's way over thirty, I don't see her the way I do other older women — boring and finished. I see her as a worldly woman. I like to work days with her because she explains things to me as if I were an adult. Unlike the nightshift nurse, Mom's friend Miss Drury, who said, 'You can't go in there, dear. Your mother wouldn't want you there,' once when I was taking ice chips to a woman in the labour room; or another time when the undertaker came to remove a patient who had passed away. I don't mind being protected from the undertaker, but I'm really curious about the labour room. Because it's all about love, birth, life.

I hate nightshift. It seems to me that most people die at night. I shiver when I come in and pass a draped gurney in the hall, waiting for undertaker Joe Driscoll. Death doesn't seem to bother Miss Drury, the way she and Joe laugh and kid around. If Joe weren't married, I'd think he and Miss Drury had something going.

It's hot, walking to work, so I'm relieved when I finally get inside the hospital where big ceiling fans whirl the air to coolness; and where, tonight, there is no draped gurney.

"Hi kiddo!" Miss Drury yells. "I'm out here." I leave my purse in the office and drag myself to a work station off the kitchen. There, when things aren't busy, we make gauze and cotton pads for bleeding maternity patients, drink coffee and talk.

"Good evening, Miss Drury." I sound like Miss Sutherland. I overheard her speaking to Miss Drury about unprofessional conduct, so I try to sound professional. Which is hard to do at night. Old Miss Drury is a real character who tells me Kettle Valley gossip and makes jokes about personal matters. Things not in line with protecting me from stuff 'your mother wouldn't like.' Once when I asked her for aspirin because I had cramps during my period, she gave me 222s, and chuckled, 'Safe again!' It took me a while to figure that one out. When I did, I used the information to tease Beth and Phoebe. They didn't think it was funny, and said they would have been worried sick if they hadn't been with older men 'who used protection.' I was embarrassed because I had to ask what they meant, but at least I found out enough not to be terrified of getting pregnant if I ever decided to go all the way.

Nightshift drags, as usual. I change two newborns, give one a bottle; Miss Drury carries the other to be breastfed. The babies are cute and cuddly, with red faces and wispy hair. I just love their little fingers and toes. After the newborns are settled, Miss Drury and I sit down in the kitchen and drink coffee boiled in a big pot with egg shells. "To hold the grounds down," she explains. She knows a lot for a practical nurse. Miss Sutherland is an RN, the real thing, but told me if I listened I could learn from Miss Drury.

Finally morning arrives. Now I'm less relieved, going off nights, because I've learned from past experience that day staff has to change beds and bathe patients.

---

I can't face going straight home, so I make a detour and stop at the river spot where Dad taught me to swim. I used to come here to cry after he died, and when Fred was reported missing. Whenever life got too hard. It's nice and quiet here now because no one is up this early. I sit on the grassy bank and watch the swift current. I love swimming in the current — the thrill of its pull — the challenge of pushing through to the far side.

I used to love the summers. Going swimming with Dad, seeing how long I could hold out against the short summer haircuts our mothers insisted upon because of the heat. We girls got what our one-and-only hairdresser called 'boyish bobs.' The poor guys got their heads shaved. Mornings we played cards, afternoons we swam. It was a lovely, lazy time.

Right now I wish I could just lie down here and go to

sleep, listening to birds and the rushing water, but I know what's ahead tonight. I turn around and make my way home.

---

Mother has everything ready, as usual. I refuse coffee, but eat a slice of toast when Mom insists, "You need nourishment so you'll be ready for the fun at the lawn dance afterwards. I ironed your pink polka dot dress last night when I couldn't sleep. I'm so edgy! This pageant is the most important event of my writing-directing career. Ironing took my mind off it and eased my nerves."

"Thanks. I'll have a bath and set my hair."

"Call me if you need help with pin curls, dearie."

"Thanks, but I won't. Beth showed me a new way she learned from a magazine. I divide my hair into four sections and wind each one up in a sock. It turns into a super page boy."

"Well, as long as it looks nice. Run along now and have a good rest."

After my bath and new hairsetting routine I fall into bed, relieved to be free of Lysol odour, although my head is uncomfortable in the bulky socks and my mind is preoccupied with Keith. With thoughts of doing it.

Flower scents and bird-songs drift in through my window.

---

"Time to get up, dear!"

*Oh. Mother. Pageant. Keith.*

I stretch in the cot, fling off the sticky sheets, and half

asleep, stumble to the bathroom. I splash cold water on my face until I feel more awake.

"Jenny? Did you hear me?"

"Yep. Coming. But I'm not hungry."

"You've got to eat," she yells. "We've a tough night ahead, both of us. I can't waste time. You get right down here!"

I know better than to cross my mother when she talks that way. I slip into my old chenille housecoat and pad barefoot down to the kitchen. Mom has set out our supper — salad, ham, bread, glasses of milk — on the shiny white oilcloth that covers our old kitchen table. 'It's easy to keep clean,' Mom always says. We only get a real tablecloth in the dining room at Christmas and other special dinners.

"Just a light meal, dearie. It's best for us both, with all the excitement."

"Right." Like other nightshift workers, I've lost my appetite. When I wake up I only want cereal or fruit. I fold a ham slice into a sandwich, eat it, and drink the milk. While Mom is upstairs, I throw my salad into the garbage-can we still call 'the chicken slop bucket,' even though we no longer keep chickens. I hate the leaf lettuce from our garden — I prefer iceberg from the store. But at least now we get white sliced bread from the States.

———

I dash upstairs to put on makeup. Mom encourages this because she wants me to be an actress, urging 'a little more colour, dear.' I often ignore her, but not tonight. I put lots of mascara on my eyelashes, eyebrow pencil on the brows, and use lots of lipstick. I can get away with lots of lipstick because I take after my dad. He was what Mom called 'Black Irish,'

with dark hair and brows. Mom was the other kind of Irish —
red hair, fair skin and freckles. She always complained about
her light eyebrows making her look 'like a peeled potato.'
She often went overboard with the eyebrow pencil, especially now that her eyesight is failing.

I inspect the results. Yes. I do look much better. In the
mirror I admire the reflection of the bronze taffeta gown
Mom laid out on my bed. Because of crowded change-facili-
ties in the high school, and because we live nearby, I'm
allowed to wear my costume from home and come back after
to change for the dance. I don't mind that at all because I like
what the laced-up dress does for me. It really pushes up my
bust, and also makes my waist look small. I imagine slinking
past Keith. But what about the back lacings?

As if reading my thoughts — some of them — Mom calls,
"I'll lace you in after I'm made up. I must look my best. I'm
prepared for a presentation, but I do wish they wouldn't
bother."

Who's she kidding? Mom loves presentations — the
speech describing her dedication to the community, someone important presenting a gift — usually special china, 'in
appreciation of all your hard work.'

I hear stomping up the porch steps and the door opening.
It's Terry in his regulation boots. Being almost family, he
doesn't have to knock.

"Hurry down, Millie," he yells. "I've brought you a tonic
to get you through your big night!"

I giggle. Mom's name is Mildred, but Terry calls her
'Millie' as a joke. The 'tonic' is a shot of rye, which she and
Terry like, and which he brings to Sunday dinner. My family
is not narrow-minded about drinking. I'm glad about that.

I've always been allowed wine at home for Christmas

and New Year's. Eighteen is under drinking age, so it's not legal until I'm twenty-one. I always refuse to drink at UBC parties, or when Tom pushes drinks at me out of the flask he takes to dances. It is also illegal to drink in night clubs where university kids go dancing, which is dumb, because all of the night clubs have bins built under tables especially for liquor bottles. People just order soft drinks for mix. Everyone knows this goes on, probably even the police, but I hate the sneakiness. I think it proper only to drink at home with my family. I'm glad I was brought up that way.

"Slip into your dress, dear," Mom commands.

I obey. I love the rustle of the stiff fabric; how it feels when it swishes around my ankles. Some of the girls have gowns with big bustles at the back. I'm sure glad I didn't fit into one of those. I hold the dress up over my head and feel it slither down my shoulders. Mother puts on her glasses so she can see the tiny hooks-and-eyes, fastening them while I hold my breath. I face myself in the mirror, Mom behind me, and can't stop admiring my own reflection.

Mother says, "You look just darling!"

"Thanks." I notice her skewed makeup. Her vision is going, and even with her new glasses I often have to rescue her before she goes out with lipstick blurred or powder spilled on her dress. I grab a tissue and clean up her smeared lipstick.

"Thanks, dear. Bifocals take getting used to." I trail behind her as she hurries down to Terry.

———————————

"Millie, you'll be breaking hearts tonight!" Terry grabs her and swings her around. It's nice, the way he teases her, because she must miss Dad, too. Although she's busy with church, choir practices, political meetings, vocal students and bridge parties, she doesn't seem to have any fun. At least Terry's visits liven things up for her.

When I swish into the kitchen Terry is pouring rye. Mom calls them 'shots' because she grew up in her stepfather's saloon and was familiar with such terms. I like it. Her worldliness is so out of keeping with how people think church choir leaders are supposed to talk. I think it's important for theatre people to sound worldly.

Terry sees me and whistles. "Wow! Won't you be the belle of the ball! Should I pour her one, Millie?"

"It won't hurt," Mom replies. "How about it, Jenny?"

"Not now. I'm too nervous. I've got to be careful with Mrs Doctor Horne's dress. Besides, I hate rye. Yech!"

"I'll fix that before the dance. After the pageant, Millie's coming back here for a nightcap. You can try my new potion then. I call it the Okanagan special because it's made with rye and apple juice."

"Okay." That would impress Keith with my sophistication; saying, 'I went home for a drink. Terry's Okanagan special.'

Mother downs her shot. "Thanks, Terry," she says. "That is just what the doctor ordered! Come on now, Jenny. I've got to be at the stage in case of last minute problems. You know how Ned Jacob counts on my support. The show must go on!" She stomps out the front door.

@CENTRE = ─────────

I follow, lifting heavy folds of brocade because I don't want to get my skirt dirty crossing the fieldpath to the school where the city has built a big outdoor platform for the pageant.

"One, two, three, testing." We hear Ned Jacob over the

public address system. Ned is the local expert on sound technicalities. He provides PA systems and loudspeakers for dances and other local events free of charge. 'Kettle Valley culture would just come to a halt without Ned Jacob,' Mom says. 'He's been such a joy to work with.'

Ned's reward tonight, for years of dedication, is to be narrator. I know that there had been a lot of angling for this role. The mayor wanted it, the MLA wanted it, the United Church minister wanted it. Mom being director had the final say, and she chose Ned. 'Not only has Ned earned it,' Mom told me, 'but it would never do to single out one religious denomination by choosing Reverend Buckman, even if he does have a splendid voice. The CCF MLA speaks at everything all the time, and Mayor Mattson plays a special role making announcements and displaying the Premier's scroll at the finale.' She spent weeks coaching Ned, night after night. I have to admit that I admire her dedication to theatre, and hope to follow her example.

She sidles up to Ned and says, "Sounds good. You'll shine tonight!" Wires from the mike trail across the school lawn and out to the platform. "Watch your feet there, Jenny," she warns.

I'm not watching my feet, I'm looking over at the gym because I hear shrieks and laughter coming from there.

"Go on ahead and join the others, dearie. Run along, now. Georgie Blake will call each act ten minutes before its turn in case people can't hear the proceedings from inside. Everyone should try to listen and not miss out on anything. You're lucky to be on at the start. That way you're able to see most of the production. I'm glad the rehearsal went badly — that's a good sign. Run along, now."

She's nervous, rambling on like that. So's Ned. He's

fiddling with wires and dials, running his hands up and down the mike.

---

As I hurry to join my group in the gym, I bump into Keith coming out of the chem lab. He looks really cute dressed in his miner's outfit — an old plaid flannel shirt, overalls and boots.

"What are you doing here?" I ask. "I thought you'd be with the olden days mining gang."

"I locked up the lab. With the school open, I had to make sure no one could wander in. There's a lot of dangerous stuff in there. You know, chemicals and equipment."

There's no 'wow,' from him, but he stares at me and blushes; rattles his keys. This reaction is encouraging.

"See you," I call, hustling inside to the gym. I don't hang around. That would be too obvious. With a mature man, subtlety is called for. My plan for Keith comes later, when we're dancing together, dancing close.

---

Beth and Phoebe hoot when they see me. There's lots of comparing and admiring each other's gowns. Our dress rehearsal hadn't been a real one for fear of damaging our costumes. We wore regular clothes in rehearsal, but spent an hour in the church basement allotting dresses and dancing a short routine under Miss Dove's eagle eyes. 'Mind your hems, girls,' she called. 'We'll just do a run-through to be certain you are able to manage the steps in costume. And for those in laced camisoles, to make sure you can breathe.' We giggled, then quickly returned to 'Uh-one, two, three step, uh-one two three glide, uh-one two three kick! And cr-oss over!'

I really love my dress. It's the prettiest one of all, I decide, after taking a good look at the others. I'm surprised to see that the bustled Dougall sisters are wearing makeup for the first time since I can remember, and that their hair is curled, not pulled back in tight knots. They're happy and excited, not the stern old maids I was always so scared of Sunday mornings when I was little.

The loudspeaker hums, going on. A record plays *O Canada*. The crowd outside sings. Inside, we all get serious and stand at attention to join in.

When the anthem ends, Ned announces that the attendance has been tallied at over three thousand people. There are cheers, applause, silence.

Ned clears his throat a couple of times before launching into the pageant introduction. His quavery voice gains strength as he describes the arrival of the first settlers in 1884. From inside we can hear the laughter when our Mayor, 'the first white male child born in Kettle Valley,' is wheeled across the stage in a baby carriage.

Georgie at the gym door calls, "Gay Nineties! You're on next!"

---

We file out and take our place beside the platform while watching a covered-wagon cross the stage. It is followed by a group of men carrying pickaxes and placer-mining pans. Ned talks about Kettle Valley's early mining settlers; its quilting bees. The local quilting group poses in a tableau before raising a banner on which is quilted, in huge gold satin letters, 50 YEARS. The crowd applauds when the quilt is placed against the backdrop.

Ned plays a record of *Alexander's Ragtime Band* after the quilters leave. Now it's our turn, as Miss Dove leads us, sashaying, onstage. Ned explains, "The miners' presence necessitated the building of saloons and the arrival of lively dancing."

This is not exactly true. Mom told me that in 'the early days' only prostitutes went out dancing and wore fancy clothes, but she left that part out of the script. If only the Misses Dougall knew! The crowd doesn't know or doesn't care. There are oh's and ah's while we do our boring old uh-one two three step, uh-one two three glide, uh-one two three kick. Nobody falls.

Just before the Doukhobor and Sons of Freedom choirs take the stage to sing their mournful *a cappella* hymns, we've left the stage and are free to mingle with the crowd to watch the performance.

———

"You look super, Jen," Tom says, clutching my arm. I smell alcohol, and feel extra pressure, a demand. He sees me sniff and says, "The guys took advantage of the jubilee to break a few rules. The cops aren't going to spoil a night that took fifty years to get here."

I know he's right, but he's staring down my neck. I clutch my hands over my chest and whisper, "Sh-h. I want to hear the Doukhobors."

I love their sad music. Tonight, Doukhobor men wear sashed tunics and pants; the women, their best shawls, aprons, and peasant skirts. I always thought Doukhobors were the most romantic aspect of life in Kettle Valley, so listen closely while Ned announces: "These pacifists who refused to bear arms for the Czar, and assisted by Count Leo Tolstoi, left Russia to create an agricultural paradise in the Kootenays."

In high school I always wished I were a Doukhobor. I wore big skirts and headscarves, and went out to visit their villages on my bike. I made friends with Doukhobor women who sold vegetables in town, and visited them. My favourite stop-over was at the home of Mrs. Chernoff, where I'd sit for hours watching one of the old women spinning wool. It seemed magic to me that the Doukhobors made everything for themselves. They spun flax into thread for crocheted table cloths. I was so impressed by these people that I even took a crack at the Cyrillic alphabet because I loved the sound of Russian, its swishy consonants.

Tom finally shuts up when the First World War act starts. I see Pete wearing his uncle's uniform, marching on with other boys to *When Johnny Comes Marching Home*. They stand, heads bowed, rifles in front of them, as Mr Morgan, who always gets drunk on Remembrance Day, plays the *Last Post*. The crowd is hushed; the Misses Dougall wipe away tears. I feel sad and begin to like them because it finally occurs to me why they never got married. That other war.

Next, the Japanese celebrate their arrival to our district in a special dance. They are wearing colourful kimonos and twirling parasols, and make me think of butterflies. When they exit, I look for my friend Sumi, but she's not there. I don't see why she couldn't have been a better sport. I would have liked to see her up there participating. Instead, she'd worked behind the scenes all day, decorating their winning parade float.

Local Second World War vets come next, looking proud

in their own uniforms, marching on to *Colonel Bogie*. They line up and sing *Roll Out the Barrel*. Then they stand at attention to salute Major Jackson, a local officer, before they make a military right turn and march off. Gosh, I wish Fred could be up there. He was a captain and deserves to participate. So do my other two brothers, but they're taking summer courses to make up time lost overseas.

Mayor Mattson strides to the mike, unfurls a scroll sent all the way from Victoria by the Premier of British Columbia. Then he reads, "Greetings to Kettle Valley on its fiftieth year of incorporation as a city, on this seventh day of August, 1947."

Next, the Mayor introduces this year's May Queen, Mary Jeffers, her escort Danny Connell, and her maids-of-honour, flower girls, and pages. I'm still bitter about never getting to be a May Queen, or even a maid-of-honour. I only got to be a flower girl, which seemed wonderful when I was six, but was not the sort of starring role I was used to at age thirteen, when I was away in Trail competing in the Kootenay Music Festival, because Mother thought the Festival was more important to my future than May Day.

Oh! Mr. Morgan is at the trumpet again. That's our cue to return for the grand finale.

———

I scurry with the others following Miss Dove onto the platform. We take our place while Ned announces, "And now for a special event, without further ado, Mayor Mattson!"

The Mayor again takes the mike to praise "Our triumphant jubilee, the many visitors from as far away as Ontario and Texas, but especially the talent shown here tonight, all due to years of devotion to our own community artists by Mrs Robert Madigan. Will Mrs Madigan please come forth to receive a token of our thanks."

Mother climbs onstage before the applauding crowd. I can't see her face, but from where I am up here I can't miss seeing the back of her good navy dress. On her left hip is a smear of what looks like face powder. She must have got it helping with makeup. A flower girl from the May Queen retinue presents her with a bouquet of carnations and a fancy-wrapped package. Mom bends down, kisses the little kid, accepts her gifts, and nods to the audience which has risen to its feet. All I can do is pray Mom won't turn and expose her powdered behind.

Ned fiddles with the record, and, his voice really strong now, announces, "Ladies and gentlemen, our National Anthem!" The crowd stiffens to attention for *God Save the King*. Mom's strong mezzo rings over the mike. At the conclusion, we all file off to go our separate ways before the dance starts.

---

Tom lurches toward me from one direction, Pete weaves from another. I smirk. Dumb drunk kids. I've outgrown them. I search for Phoebe and Beth, and in turning, discover that my long skirt swirls. I wish I'd known that earlier, when I met Keith in the doorway.

Phoebe and Beth wave from the school where they went to change for the lawn dance. I'm starving for food and thirsting for my drink. Walking home helps me avoid Tom and Pete, who'll probably have found other partners before I get back.

It's cool now, and the stars are out. At times like this I

usually like to stroll down by the river, watching the moon's rippled reflection. But not tonight. Not yet, not alone.

———————

I hear our local orchestra, The Monashee Melodeers, starting up. Miss Vickers pounds piano, Ned plays clarinet, Don Morgan beats drums. The Monashee Melodeers have played at local dances ever since I was allowed to go. At my first high school mixer; my first formal. The Melodeers even played at dances when my parents went to the New Year's Eve Ball and to legion and lodge dances. It's not a good orchestra, but it's all we've got, and what it lacks in musical quality it makes up for with memories and a strong beat. It always adds a couple of 'new hits' to its repertoire each year. This year, it's banging out tunes from *Oklahoma*!

Music follows me off the grounds, across the field, and up our creaking old porch stairs. When I reach the door I'm so tired I could drop. Terry is in the kitchen opening the apple juice. He turns when I slam the door, and calls, "Come on and try my special!"

"Not yet. I've got to go upstairs and change."

"Try one before you go up. It's nice and cold."

It sounds good, and I'm thirsty. I slouch into the kitchen. Terry fills two tumblers and hands me one. "Try this!"

I clutch the glass and drink. All I taste is apple juice. I gulp it down, mindful of Mrs Doctor Horne's dress, and set the glass on a shelf. I'm so hungry that I open the icebox to see what's left for a snack. Cheese, tomatoes, lettuce. Perfect.

Terry asks, "Doesn't that go down smooth?"

"Yes," I agree, "it does. I'll have another when I come back." I pause, wondering how long I'll have to wait until Mom comes home. I could miss half the dance. It's going to be so beautiful, outdoors under the stars. I want to get back there before Keith leaves. Terry is like a brother...why not? "Could you do me a favour?" I ask him. "Just unhook the back. Mom laced me in, and I can't get this dress over my head to change for the dance unless you'll help." "Easy," he says, "Turn around." I'm comfortable with him now, and don't feel embarrassed when he fumbles with the back of my dress, although I do clutch the bodice against me during the unlacing and unbuttoning and when I dart away upstairs, although by then he's too busy mixing another drink to look.

---

I hear Mom come in, breathless. She calls, "Jenny, can you believe it? Royal Albert cups and saucers, my favourite!" "Lovely!" I yell. "I'll admire them when I come down."

I stand on the braided bedroom carpet and slide out of the beautiful antique dress. I place it on its quilted hanger, wrap it in tissue paper, fold it into a big box. I'm relieved and sad to be free of it. It made me feel special for a while. Not the dance, just the dress. I feel like crying. I take a deep breath and put on my pink polka dot dress. The polka dots seem to be getting all blurry. It's just tiredness from coming off nightshift, I guess.

Sandals or heels? I've had enough bloody discomfort for one night. Sandals.

---

I hear Terry and Mom downstairs knocking back shots. When I get down, I can see that Mom is flushed and smiling. I guess this pageant was a big thing for her, being stuck in

Kettle Valley. I wander into the dining room and exclaim over her china before joining them in the kitchen.

"I told Millie I'd volunteer to handle the other ladies' costumes if they need help," Terry joshes.

"I'm glad he was here to help you out, Jen," she says. "I wouldn't want you to have waited. I had a devil of a time getting away, but I'm going back." She kicks off her good shoes, wriggles her broad feet.

I open the icebox. Terry says, "I told Millie I gave you a drink, because she gave her permission earlier. She told me you could have another."

"She's earned it," Mother says. "All those practices after working so hard in that hospital. She's a good little sport."

I halt in front of the icebox. I don't like being called 'a good little sport.' I don't like the idea of Terry and Mom *allowing* me to have a drink as though I'm just a kid. I slam shut the icebox door. "I'll take that drink. Make it strong. I couldn't even taste the rye."

Mom winks at Terry, who adds more rye. I hate it when Mom winks — something she used to do with my dad when they shared a secret that left me out. I down my drink. She slides back into her shoes and calls, "See you at the dance!" She hustles out the hall.

Now Terry winks and adds two more shots to my empty glass. Then he tops it with apple juice. "I know you're grown up, kid."

*Kid.* The idiot thinks he understands but doesn't hear how he really sounds.

I'll show them both. I'm determined to drink all this to get even with Mom for belittling me, and with Terry for treating me like a baby. Besides, I've lost my appetite and apple juice is as good as a meal.

When I stalk off, Terry yells, "Save me a dance, kid!"
I yell back, "If you're lucky, old man!"

———————

Golly! I'm no longer tired, no longer careful, free of that tight old dress and high heels. But I'm getting dizzier and dizzier. I guess it's all the excitement. I run through the fields and trip. After getting up I shout, "Tonight I'm going to do it! Tonight I'm losing my virginity!"

Tom has been waiting for me near the schoolyard, and he grabs me, chuckling, "Well Miss Self-Righteous, what's gotten into you? You smell like a distillery and roll like a ship in a storm!"

"I do not! That smell is my new perfume. Darn it! I should have used more perfume, or have rinsed my mouth with it, the way Scarlett did.

"Whoa, girl," Tom chuckles. "You nearly fell again." He grabs me. I ignore him and kick off my sandals.

"The grass feels so-o wonderful! You've no idea what it's like, wearing bloody shoes all the time!"

"Everybody wears shoes," Tom replies. "I wear shoes."

"But you can sit down. At a desk or in the truck." I wriggle my feet in the grass. This dumb foot and mouth talk has distracted me from my plan. "Where's Keith? Have you seen him?"

"Old teach? Nowhere. Probably the spoilsport has gone home. Or inside to protect his precious school property."

I break away from Tom, lurch through the crowd, yelling, "Keith! Keith!"

Everything is spinning and exciting. Why is everyone laughing? Pete spots me. I see him coming my way just as Keith reaches out to break my fall.

Keith's face is red. He's not smiling. "Oh my gosh!" he says.

"Take me into the lab!" I demand. "I'll explain it. About losing my virginity."

"That's a good idea. Come on." He grabs my arms from behind as though he expects me to struggle. People watch and smile. It's so nice the way everyone is happy and friendly, and Keith is so eager to be alone with me.

———————

He takes me into the school. Near the lab he lets go of me while he finds his key. I flop against the wall. "Hold on," he begs. "Be a good girl."

"I don't want to be a good girl! I'm tired of being a good girl! I want to lose my virginity! I want to do something special to celebrate the Golden Jubilee!" I fling my arms around him while he opens the door. He reaches out, grabs my arms and pushes me into the lab. He slams the door.

"There." He lets me go again while he switches on the light. The lab dazzles and the long shiny work tables make me squint. I turn off the switch and blurt, "It's too bright. It hurts my eyes and everyone will know." I reach for his belt and try to unbuckle it; he wrenches away.

"What are you trying to do, for heaven's sake?" he asks.

I giggle. "We've got to undress! I'm too old to be a virgin. I'm the only virgin I know! I want to do it with you."

"No you don't. I'm taking you home. Please, be a good girl!"

I cry. "I'm sick of being a good girl! I've heard it my whole life! 'The little Madigan girl, the good little Madigan girl'!" I fall against him and whimper, "What's wrong with me, Keith? Don't you like me?"

"I do...I'm...you're...I had to do something or that Tom...he's a real wolf...people heard..."

I lean against him. He feels nice. His chest, his rough shirt. Dizzy, I nestle in.

"I can't let you spoil your mother's big night."

I pull away, pound his chest with my fists yelling, "All you care about is my mother!"

"Sh-h. I care about you or I wouldn't be here. People out there saw us. They'll wonder. They'll talk. I'm a teacher...Gosh, the principal..." He frowns and rubs his battered chest. "Wait," he says. "I'll be right back." When he lets me go I flop against the wall. When he leaves, he locks me in.

It will happen! He's gone to get it. Protection. I should be ready. I fumble out of my dress, panties and bra. It's so nice and cool...being naked. I grope for the light switch...can't find it...he'll take care of everything...men do. When I hear The Melodeers striking up, I join in and sing, "Peo—ple will say we're in lo—ve!"

---

*Footsteps in the hall. My lover. Must welcome him. Door opens. Lights flash on.* It's Miss Sutherland.

"Dear God!" she blurts.

I clutch my arms around my body and mumble, "Where's Keith? What's happening? Did you come here to fire me?"

"Nobody will fire you. Someone gave you too much to drink, so Keith asked me to take you home. Put your clothes on," she commands, holding out my bra and panties. I obey. Then, "Here, Keith found your sandals."

I slide into them, whimpering, "I just wanted to lose my virginity."

"So we all heard. You're lucky Keith rescued you. Let me see…I know, I'll take you out the back way. Here's your dress."

I fumble into it. The dots on it keep moving and make me feel funny. Miss Sutherland grabs my arm and leads me down the hall and out the door.

As soon as the cool air hits, I feel worse, and when we reach the field I fall on the grass, vomiting.

"Good. That'll get some alcohol out of your system."

I keep on vomiting. Sour, liquid apple-ish vomit. Miss Sutherland sits beside me, holds my head, wipes my face with her handkerchief. Finally I say, "I'm a bit better. I want to get home…but Mom…"

"She's staying on at the party to enjoy the festivities." She helps me up, holding my hand until we reach our house.

---

We're in the kitchen. On the counter is the empty rye bottle and an apple juice tin. Just seeing them makes me sick. Miss Sutherland takes a bottle of ginger ale out of the icebox and fills a glass. "Drink this," she says.

I sip ginger ale. She hands me two pills. "Get these down. One is Vitamin B, and the other is a prescription painkiller. Believe me, Miss Madigan, I've had experience treating hangovers. The boys coming back from leave…"

The bulb hanging from the ceiling seems brighter than usual, our kitchen floor more slanted. I swallow the pills, drink more ginger ale. Miss Sutherland faces me, holds my shoulders.

"Go on upstairs now. You're steadier, and you look

better. You can manage. I'm going back to the celebration as if none of this had happened. Remember that. I expect you at work tomorrow at seven o'clock sharp." She's gone.

---

Light streams through the window and stabs my eyes. My head throbs. I moan and duck under the covers. How to get out of work? *Last night...yelling about losing my virginity...people laughing...Tom groping...oh no! Keith in the lab!* Where to hide? Where to go? Not to work, no. *Miss Sutherland. Vomiting. 'Seven o'clock sharp.'*

"Jenny! Breakfast is ready. You're changing shifts today! Miss Sutherland reminded me in case you forgot. She told me she's counting on you."

I drag myself out of bed into the bathroom. Where's my nightgown? How come I'm only in bra and panties? Oh...*'You can manage.'*

I never want to see Keith again...or Miss Sutherland...so nice...promised not to fire me...got to get to work. I owe her that.

I douse my head with cold water and twist an elastic around my wet hair into a pony tail. I don't like what I see in the mirror. My face is pale and there are big dark circles under my eyes. I fumble with lipstick and give up. I don't really care, so go back to my room. My stomach heaves and my head throbs.

After I put on my white uniform, shoes and stockings, I start to feel better. Sort of. Disguised. Respectable-looking.

---

I stumble downstairs, relieved not to smell coffee. The very thought of it makes me sick. I watch Mom. How much does she know? What has she heard?

Nothing, given her big smile. "What a night! Do you realize that your own mother didn't get in until after 2 a.m.! I met some oldtimers, and we got reminiscing. And of course, everyone kept coming up to congratulate me.

"That Miss Sutherland from the hospital seems very nice for a newcomer. She worried that the evening upset you, coming off nightshift. *Insisted* tea would be better for you this morning, and a light breakfast. Although I appreciate her taking an interest in you, I hope she's not filling your head with ideas about going into nursing. That's not what I had in mind for you after devoting years coaching you in drama, and after your theatre triumph in Vancouver. I've always dreamt of a theatre career for you, carrying on the Madigan name in theatre, after me."

I sip tea, eat dry toast and jam. Mother rambles on. *'Hospital work will give you a dose of reality. Bedpans, death, the seamy side...'*

My chair scrapes our worn-out linoleum when I stand. The sound grates my nerves. Mom sees me wince.

*'That Miss Sutherland was right. You are under a strain. But you've handled major performances and starring roles. I think it must be that dreadful job, dearie.*

*'For me, Jenny, it's all over. There'll be nothing like last night for another fifty years so I made the most of it! You come right home if that job is too much. You're just beginning, your whole life is ahead of you...I was proud of Ned. He did well.'*

Ramble, ramble.

I frown when she kisses my cheek, then slump into my

collar hunching my shoulders, trying to be invisible as I slouch out the door.

———————

I'll never, ever, live last night down. Local people really only care about what happens here. Nobody in Kettle Valley even read about me in *The Vancouver Province*. Big city people expect actresses to behave wildly. Small town people are too isolated from culture to appreciate artists like me.

I've lost everything, even my ability to march. During the war when girls were in cadets, I was a platoon leader, just because of my march. It was my trademark. The boys teased me, but not Mrs. MacDonald. 'Keep that stride, Jenny. You've an assertive walk that people take seriously.' How have the mighty fallen. I'll never be taken seriously again.

Walking downhill by the slough I smell wild flowers, a smell I usually love. Today it's sickening. So are thoughts of mushrooms growing there, mushrooms I usually rush to pick after the rain before anyone else gets them.

A car honks and slows down. I hear Tom call, "Need a lift? We have to pick up where we left off." He opens his car door. I brace myself, make an effort to regain the Jenny Madigan stride, and yell, "Buzz off!"

"You are nasty, the day after. You'll be glad of a date tonight." He slams the door. The motor starts, the Forestry truck roars past.

Across the street, shrouded in trees, is the courthouse, a building that has terrified me my whole life. When I was really little, someone told me that the jail was in there, where they locked up bad people. After hearing that I crossed the street whenever I neared the courthouse. I still do. Now I

think all those years of terror foretold my downfall last night.
I belong in jail.

---

My stomach heaves when I pass through the big iron
gates at the hospital entrance. I dawdle on my way up the
concrete stairs, because inside everyone knows. The doctors
laughed last night when I passed them screaming about
losing my virginity; so did Miss Dwyer who called, 'Atta
girl!' whirling by in Ned Driscoll's arms. Miss Sutherland
saw me naked, watched me vomit.

The big front door seems heavier than usual. When I
bring my purse to the office, Miss Sutherland is inspecting
charts. "Good morning, Miss Madigan," she says, as if it were
just any other day.

"Good morning, Miss Sutherland." I'm waiting for something. I don't know what. Something bad.

"Before you begin work, take these." She hands me two
pills like the ones she gave me last night. "There's lemonade
in the kitchen. Be sure to drink a full glass. You are probably
dehydrated." She returns to the charts. "You'll be working
with Miss Sookocheff today."

I'm relieved. That wasn't so bad. And I like working with
Annie Sookocheff. She's from the Sons of Freedom, and so
strict she doesn't go to movies or read what she calls 'junk,'
meaning movie magazines. But last summer she introduced
me to Tolstoi, a writer not on Kettle Valley High's curricu-
lum, or even yet, in any of my UBC English courses. Now that
I think of it, I realize it was Annie who introduced me to
Chekhov, which gave me an edge when I auditioned for *The
Three Sisters*. Annie doesn't go to dances, and she wasn't
onstage singing with the Sons of Freedom last night, so there

will be no teasing from her. Just our usual talk about patients, and if I ask, about her religion. We can call each other by first names because we're only nurse's aides, not even practical nurses. Miss Sutherland says Annie has the makings of a 'truly fine nurse,' and regrets that her religion kept her from attending school. When I asked Annie about this she told me it was 'to avoid contamination.' This morning, I think the Sons of Freedom aren't so weird after all.

Annie gets to do a lot of responsible jobs — to help out in the labour room, prepare dead patients for the undertaker. I feel a bit jealous when I hear the doctors ask, 'Where's Miss Sookocheff?' if they're really busy and need assistance. I can't help but resent them taking her more seriously than me, a university student, but think it's because I have to live down being 'the good little Madigan girl.' When I told Annie about this, it was the first time I ever saw her really laugh. She said, 'Yeah. I've nothing to live down except nude protests and my parents being jailed.'

"Good morning." Annie smiles and is so sparkly in her white uniform that I can't stand looking at her. "We're starting in there," she announces, nodding at the men's ward over an armful of fresh linen. She must have got here early again.

"Okay. I'll be with you after I get back from the kitchen."

---

Now, on to face the cook, Mrs Bogdan, who waltzed past me at the dance.

"You're walking a bit straighter this morning," she chuckles. "You really tied one on last night! I was telling the doctors this morning, when good little girls let go, they're the worst. Still waters, you know." She shakes her head. "That

Tom fella had to hold you up, then the teacher. By the way, where *did* you two get to?"

"The teacher was explaining chemistry to me in the lab."

Mrs. Bogdan snorts, "Chemistry? So that's what they call it these days."

I hold out my glass. "May I have some lemonade, please?"

She fills my glass from a fresh pitcher she's made. "Lemonade is the best thing going, take it from me." She lowers her voice. "I'm experienced with hangovers. Doctors are the worst. It's the strain. I figure with all their responsibilities, they need to cut loose once in a while."

I swallow the pills, hurry to join Annie in such a rush that I bump into the new doctor from Ireland, Dr Ryan.

"Whoa there, Miss Madigan," he says. "You're a hazard to the medical staff. I've a baby to deliver, so don't knock me down. I must say I admire your stamina." He lowers his voice, and offers, "I've the very remedy if you find yourself, well, feeling under par."

"I feel just fine, thank you. And I've got work to do myself, if you'll please excuse me."

"There now, I meant no harm, Miss Madigan. Don't be taking offense. Just listen to an experienced Irish doctor. By your name and habits I take you to be one of our own, and believe me lass, when it comes to drink we Irish are the worst. I'm an expert. If you'll forgive me, I saw you having a grand time and all last night, and much as I wished I were young again myself, I feared for you today. Facing the snickering world and all, while feeling poorly to boot. I'd be no help with the shame. That's Father Moore's department, but I've some pills that are just the ticket—"

"Painkillers and B vitamins. I've had some! And I'm

United Church, thank you very much," I explode. "Everyone in this bloody hospital is an expert." Dr Ryan chuckles and charges down the hall, just as I think, That was no way to talk to a doctor! I should apologize, but Annie is waiting, and Dr Ryan has already disappeared.

---

My head keeps throbbing, but the day goes quickly because there's so much work to do. When Annie and I change beds, she lifts patients while I spread clean sheets under them. We fold perfect mitred corners the way Miss Sutherland taught us. Thank heavens most of the men in here are well enough to bathe themselves. Only two — one a fracture patient, the other an old senile guy — need our help.

The fracture patient is a Doukhobor. He complains, but Annie quiets him with a smile and a few words in Russian. The other old man, an English man, is too far gone to understand anything, and always throws off the sheet, lifts his gown to expose his withered thing. It looks like a rotting parsnip. I turn away, but Annie accepts his action calmly. I guess, being a Doukhobor, she accepts nudity as perfectly natural. It's part of her religion. It's not as if I'm immature or inexperienced or anything. It's just the different way we Canadians were raised. Today, particularly, I'm relieved to find that the English man has been cleaned up. He must have soiled his bed during the early morning of nightshift, when changing his bed and bathing him was a job Miss Drury did to protect my innocence. On days, when she's not there, I have to clean up his mess. It always makes me sick to my stomach.

---

By lunch hour, much as I dread sitting down to face the rest of the staff, I'm starving. Everyone will be there except the doctors who eat at home, and Annie who grew up vegetarian and can't stand being around meat. She brings her own lunch of cheese or egg sandwiches out to the back steps and eats in the sunlight. I'd like to go with her, the way I usually do, but I smell roast beef and potatoes and can't resist. No wonder. Yesterday I hardly ate a thing.

"It's time to bring the trays out," Annie tells me. "Let's go."

We wash our hands before going to the kitchen for the trays all neatly arranged and tagged by Mrs Bogdan. We carry them out to the wards, putting them on stands that swing over the beds. We crank the mattresses up so patients can sit to eat. Annie takes the special tray with a salad plate of devilled eggs and vegetables to the Doukhobor. He looks around at the other trays and smells the beef. I cut up the beef, but Annie takes over and feeds the senile guy while I bring trays to the other wards. After we break, she goes outside.

———————

I have to face Mrs Bogdan, Miss Sutherland, and Miss Armour at the big linen-covered table. Miss Sutherland sits at the head, serving us like a family.

Miss Armour always acts resentful, because, although only a practical nurse, she was the matron for years. Until there were new Provincial laws passed that required that a Registered Nurse head the staff. This change caused a community uproar. Miss Armour was United Church, and the whole congregation was ready to petition the government about outsiders taking over the hospital.

The petition never got started after Miss Sutherland arrived. Though Anglican, she was backed up by legion members because of her war record. For a while, Dr Ryan being Irish and RC was a community target, but the other doctors said they'd quit and close the hospital if they didn't have help to share their load. Mom told me she heard that Father Moore made a special sermon to his parish about how important it was to have their own Catholic doctor, so most of Holy Cross switched to Dr Ryan. He was good at obstetrics, which not only made a big hit with the Catholics, but with the other doctors who hated getting up in the middle of the night just for babies. They used to leave night deliveries for Miss Drury. Pretty soon people stopped gossiping about 'the Irish not fighting at our side,' and anyone in Kettle Valley with an Irish ancestor was inviting Dr Ryan for dinner. He was young and good-looking, so I figured he was seen as a suitable husband for a Catholic girl. Like Miss Sutherland, Dr Ryan settled in. But Miss Armour still acts mad about only being assistant matron.

"I loved watching the Japs dancing," Miss Armour says, spearing a roast potato. "They looked so cute in their pretty little outfits. As long as they know their place and live outside the city, I've nothing against them. It's too bad your friend Sumi didn't show some spirit and participate. I guess she's one of those who think they're above us. There are people like that in every race."

I pick up my knife and slash at a slice of beef. I too, wish that Sumi had danced. When I asked her about it she changed the subject. When I asked her again, she told me she was waiting for a permit from the city to get a job. She can't go to the west coast to UBC because of the war, even though it's over. She told me that she'd waited a whole day in the City Office, then was informed to come back and wait again.

Japanese girls can only take certain jobs downtown, as housemaids or nurses, because Kettle Valley people don't want them working in the city. They are only allowed to work as farm labourers on the outskirts of town.

Sumi led our class when we were in Junior Matric. I wasn't too pleased, because she was the first person to get a higher mark than me in English. That was before I got to know her. Now one of the new lawyers wants to hire her as a secretary, and all the council members are up in arms about it. When I told Fred what happened to her at the City Office, he got mad and went straight to City Hall and told the council that kind of treatment was what he'd been fighting against, not what he'd been fighting for. Nobody took him seriously because of his combat fatigue. They just said, 'Thanks, Fred. We'll talk it over.'

"The band was super, playing those new tunes," Old Armour continues. "Didn't you think so Jenny?"

I finish chewing beef and gravy, swallow, nod, take another mouthful.

Armour rattles on, "You've got a big appetite for some-one who —"

"Is so young and healthy," Miss Sutherland adds. "A good sign, Miss Madigan."

Mrs Bogdan winks at me. I'm still sawing and mashing and chewing, but I'm so grateful to her for shutting up Armour that I stop long enough to say, "You're a fantastic cook, Mrs Bogdan. I wish my mom could cook like this."

"Your mother's mind is on higher things, dear," Old Armour chimes in. "She's an artistic, rather than practical soul. You should be grateful for all the years she devoted to teaching you drama and singing. Always giving you the best leading roles—"

Miss Sutherland snaps, "Cooking, too, is an art. We're all grateful to Mrs Bogdan. It is important to have someone aware of what goes on in a kitchen."

Miss Drury told me that Mrs Bogdan had applied for a job as cook when Miss Armour was in charge, but wasn't hired then because she was living common-law. After Miss Sutherland took over, she hired Mrs Bogdan.

I resist mopping up gravy with Mrs Bogdan's homemade bread and push back my chair. "Excuse me, Miss Sutherland. May I skip dessert? I hear Annie coming in. If we start now we can clear the trays and finish upstairs together."

"Excellent. Although I for one, will never say no to Mrs Bogdan's superb chocolate cake. But you must have more lemonade. In hot weather it's important to replenish fluids."

I drink a small glass of lemonade. Mrs Bogdan beams and says, "I'll save a couple of pieces of cake and leave them in the fridge for you and Annie."

"Thanks."

---

Annie strolls in, carefully places wax paper and crusts in the garbage, folding the paper first. I watch her, and think, *she's so neat.* Sometimes I can't stand her.

"Let's get going, Annie," I tell her. We carry and stack trays, fill water jugs for the afternoon, straighten patients' beds. Some patients are dozing and resent being disturbed; others are chatty and want to visit.

All I want to do is just get through the afternoon while trying to think of some way to get out of returning Mrs Doctor Horne's dress to her myself. How can I face her, after screaming past her last night? Maybe Miss Dove could take it back. *No.* I remember *her* shocked face when Keith led me staggering across the schoolyard. How come I remember all this? I thought drunks blacked out or something. It would be easier if I could do that. Black out.

What will Pete think? Now even he won't want to be seen with me. I saw him watching and frowning, over at the side under some trees, with Phoebe and Beth. He's a nice boy and our mothers belong to the same church group.

Worst of all, I keep thinking about how I acted with Keith, and my face burns, I'm so ashamed. What if he hadn't sent Miss Sutherland after me?

"It's nearly quitting time, Jenny. We're through. I've chores at home, and a long bike ride home to the colony."

*I'm confused...Oh. Annie.*

"You go on," I suggest. "Mrs Bogdan left us chocolate cake in the fridge. I don't want mine, so please take it. I think I'll hang around and find something else to do here."

"What's wrong, are you sick?" she asks. Usually she's the one to volunteer for extra duties. The one Miss Sutherland describes as having 'willing shoulders.' Now she says, "Thanks for your cake. Are you sure you're okay?"

I am sick. My stomach churns and my head throbs. Worse than that, I'm afraid to leave the hospital and face everyone outside. The staff wasn't too bad. They're over with. Now I feel safe here, and that the hospital is my hiding place.

Because I know the Kettle Valley grapevine. People who didn't even see me will have heard about me. Over the telephone, over fences, in stores. Mom says they should print gossip in *The Courier* and get it over with.

Annie just stands there, waiting for me to answer.

"No. I'm not sick. Just let-down. The Jubilee being over and everything. Practices were a nuisance, but now there won't be much to do all summer."

"Okay, then. I'll go." But she doesn't move, just stays put, frowning. "You're funny, Jen. You complained about practices ever since they started. Now you can do whatever you want after work and you still complain. What about that guy Tom? The one with the truck? Or Pete, who's really cute, if you don't mind my saying so."

"I'm fed up with those kids. They're boring. I think I'll just stay home and read."

"Time to go, you two." Miss Sutherland enters the ward. "You've both worked hard and done well as usual. Be careful riding your bike on the highway, Miss Sookocheff, and crossing the river in the basket bridge. Miss Madigan, I'd like a word with you. Please drop into my office before you leave."

"Yes, Miss Sutherland." She is going to fire me after all. That's it. The hospital board got together, discussed my disgrace, and have already phoned her. But that would not be so bad. I could go back to Vancouver, get a waitress job and escape everything. Then I'd have nothing to live down and could get back in the drama group. But poor Mom.

"Bye," Annie calls, running off down the corridor. "See you tomorrow!"

"Okay." *Maybe.*

---

I stall before bracing myself for the worst, then head for Miss Sutherland's office.

She crosses the room to shut the door. "Sit down there, please, Miss Madigan." I slump into a chair across from her desk.

She returns to her desk, sits down and faces me. No frown. No smile. What's up?

"How do you feel?" she inquires. "Stomach and head any better?"

I shake my head. "I was okay most of the morning, but it's all coming back now. The headache, my stomach…but the worst thing is, I'm remembering everything!"

"Good. I mean, about remembering. Let's hope your memory will help you be more cautious with alcohol in the future, now that you've learned how it affects your judgment."

"I know for sure I'll never drink again as long as I live, although that decision can't change what happened last night. Everyone else will remember, too!" I let go, and cry. She passes me a box of tissues.

"Yes, they will remember. With humour, most of them. They are also remembering the pageant. You were not exactly the whole show. They're still talking about the mayor in his baby carriage, the marvellous Russian choirs, all your mother's hard work, and the splendid parade floats.

"Surely you realize that everyone behaves indiscreetly at some time. It's not how foolishly one behaves, but what one learns from misbehaviour. You were very lucky. Keith is a responsible person, and others are determined to protect your mother from knowing what happened. She's been through enough. Your father's death, Fred's disability, her other two boys overseas. Those same people also realize that this distress was hard on you. Kettle Valley people, like most people, are kind souls." She pauses. "About some things. Particularly when it comes to its early settlers. They'll allow a native daughter one silly adventure."

"And if I stay out of sight, they'll forget. I've decided to stay home from tonight's lake dance—"

"Oh no you don't! That would be the worst possible thing

to do, adding cowardice to shame. Why, I'm disappointed! I thought you had more gumption. Listen to me. *This is an order.* You must go back out there, go to the dance with your friends, face people and show them what Jenny Madigan is made of!"

"But they'll laugh!"

"They have and they will. What's wrong with laughter? Don't tell me you've never laughed at others, because I've heard you."

*The back row fogies.*

"You'll make more mistakes, if you're human, and learn from them if you are intelligent." She stands up. "About your head. Here." She gives me two more pills. "Take these with fruit juice or ginger ale before you go home. Have a rest, eat some supper, telephone your friends and decide what you're going to wear tonight. Smile and have fun even if you have to pretend. I'm told you're a fine actress. Here's your chance to prove it. I'll see you tomorrow at seven o'clock, as usual." She sits down and takes out some charts, a signal for me to wipe my eyes and get going.

"Thank you, Miss Sutherland," I say as I leave.

---

Closing her door I think, that wasn't so bad. I clutch the tablets, take them out to the kitchen and pour orange juice into a tumbler. I gulp it down with the pills. A pill sticks in my throat, gritty and acrid. I wash it down with more juice.

I lean against the sink, stalling my move outside. Remember, *This is an order.* I straighten up, take a deep breath, and go.

I deliberately cross the street to walk beside the courthouse, bound for the river. I'm determined to stand tall, in the Jenny Madigan march, but find myself slinking.

I'm relieved when I finally reach the Kettle. There are little kids splashing and swimming; families setting out their Saturday picnics on blankets. They don't even notice me.

Their happiness makes me feel worse. I seriously think about death by drowning. Virginia Woolf did it. Mrs. Mac-Donald told us all about that in English class. How Virginia just walked into the Ouse river. What would it be like, not to fight the current, to allow it to pull me under? No, I could never do that, because I love this river too much. And it would tarnish my father's memory. There are other ways. Maybe I could pinch some pills at work. Darn it. That's out too. They'd only blame 'that' Miss Sutherland. How will I ever live this down?

What is it Fred always tells me whenever I go to him with my troubles? Oh yes. 'In fifty years, nobody will give a goddam.'

In fifty years Mother won't be alive. She won't be here to put on the pageant. Maybe there won't even be a pageant. Maybe Kettle Valley will be a ghost town like Eholt. Maybe I won't be alive. If I am, I'd be older than the Dougall sisters. Golly, just thinking of all this stuff makes me feel worse. A lot sadder.

———————

I wonder which dress I should wear to the dance. I know! I'll wear the slinky one Madge passed down to me. It's green and backless, so it will show off my tan.

'Jenny Madigan swimming with her dad.'

'Kettle Valley.'

'Annie and her baby son.'

'Jenny's Junior Matric class'

'Sumi.'

'The station.'

# The Centennial: 1997

Thank heavens I made it to the bus. I push my way into line and buy a Senior's return ticket to Kettle Valley. My last hurdle. I was afraid I'd never survive this trip. Not that I don't enjoy travel. I do. I was always a great traveller. Brazil, Cuba, Spain, Italy, Ireland. I did them all, those countries. Even lived in some of them. And when I was young, had ecstatic love affairs in 'faraway places with strange-sounding names.'

Ecstatic, I suppose, because of the format. A short limited run. Settings: foreign; scenes: café, bedroom, airport; cast: naïve Canadian college teacher, exotic local hero; props: table, chairs, bed, strong dark coffee before strong dark coffee became trendy, bottles of wine; costumes: minimal in the tropics, heavy knits in Ireland.

My travels and love affairs gave me a facility with foreign languages and international cuisine. I've read, recently, that learning languages and having new experiences help prevent Alzheimer's. Not that I looked that far ahead in those days, or that anyone had ever heard of Alzheimer's back then. But yes, my cultural interactions and learning experiences, have kept me more alert than my contemporaries.

No more light romances for me now, unfortunately, although remembering them, I do always think they would have made charming musicals. Just charming. During my travels people laughed because I always mentioned something that reminded me of BC. In Cuba, I exclaimed over tropical fruit and flowers, 'It's like the Okanagan!' In Brazil's parched sertão, I said, 'This reminds me of Osoyoos.' Ireland became my second home when I lived in the village of Duncannon, where I told my neighbours it was just like living in Kettle Valley, and that Waterford's estuary was similar to Vancouver's West End.

Back then, gallant men used to be eager to carry my baggage, or there were helpful porters. That was before political correctness — feminism, agism, all the other 'isms.' Nowadays a man probably fears being swatted with a purse or a lawsuit if he shows a woman courtesy. So here I am lining up for a two-bit trolley. I slide in a quarter, yank out my baggage-laden trolley, and wreck my seventy-year-old shoulders.

———————

What I find most difficult about travel now are all the transitions. Leave home for airport; airport for destination, then to hotel or bus or train. All those hurdles make me feel like a steeplechase rider afraid of missing a jump. But it's very much worse, going home.

*Imagine that. Me calling BC home after fifty years away.*

Oh yes, transitions, especially travelling west. Not sleeping the night before because I'm afraid of missing my flight on some no-name charter demanding my presence at the airport two hours before departure. Ho! That means arising at 4 A.M. and taking a bloody cab.

I have a secret fear of never returning from flights to BC. Perhaps this is because recently I've only gone back for funerals, those confrontations with my own mortality. At this time of one's life, grief is doubled. I not only experience people I love leaving me, but must also face the loss of eventually leaving people I love. My children and grandchildren, nieces and nephews. Friends. Sort of advance grief. I believe they call it preparatory grief. I remember reading about something like that. Or else I've gone back home to attend a horrendous reunion and been exiled for betraying my family by settling Back East and becoming a New Democrat. A second exile, like the exile of age.

First hurdle this time, was: Get to airport, get cleared, and wait in the departure lounge. At least this trip, I was able to choose a window seat. For me, this is important. Landscape always was. I love watching little squares of Ontario vanish; seeing the sun blush on clouds; then, Rockies — *Mountains*. Vancouver. Blue. Ocean. Sky.

In the past I always stayed with Phoebe, who met me at Vancouver airport, talked non-stop about her love affairs and her newest best-selling romance novel. Phoebe, the most unlikely of our high school gang, who actually did become famous. That is, if one has low literary standards. Her recent letters have not been about plot outlines or huge advances, but about osteoporosis, her cholesterol count, and her personal trainer Lars, who has her lifting weights. That's another problem I have with my contemporaries. They are all so preoccupied with their physical conditions. I find ill-health a

tedious topic, so make an effort to cultivate young people.
This Lars, Phoebe wrote in her last letter, 'is a Swede with
pecs and glutes that are a joy to behold.'

Visiting Phoebe was always fun. She'd meet me at the
airport and drive me to her condo near The Sylvia. She
always baked me a BC salmon and took me swimming in her
pool. I slept in her guest suite with its own bathroom. Next
day after breakfast she'd drive me to the airport, ferry docks,
or bus station. Wherever. I must say she remained very
easygoing and natural for a celebrity. Made time for people
like me. Her dear old friends.

This trip, Phoebe and Lars are off in the States, getting
into shape at the Pritikin Institute. So after my leaving-
Toronto hurdle I had to get through all the other transitions
on my own. Pick up luggage at airport, snag a taxi to Sand-
man Hotel; sleep, breakfast; then, burdened with baggage,
run across the street to wait in the rain for a local bus.

---

I'm a Type-A personality and run for buses even if I know
I'm twenty minutes ahead of schedule. You just never know.
That's always been my way, so I'm never late. Catch that bus!
Get that guy! There will never be another one this way. I
suppose I'm not only a Type-A, I'm a pessimist.

I arrived at the Pacific Coachlines terminal an hour early.
My daughters always make fun of me for being early, but it's
a relief for me. Especially now, for this will be a long ride. At
my age exercise is important before lengthy sedentary travel:
so is getting out at stops. Now I have time to walk around the
terminal, keeping a close eye on my luggage. Eventually I
saunter over to grab a couple of those little free cartons of
apple juice. Apple juice. That reminds me…

Oh! They're already boarding! I pick up another carton and ask the driver about my suitcase. This is the first time I've ever checked my bags since I went to Rome for Easter Week in a Holy Year and arrived in Rome wearing an orange poncho and slacksuit. That was it. The elegant clothes in my luggage somehow landed in Madrid. That experience would have been humiliating for me, if Italian men weren't so gallant. Not that His Holiness gave a sweet goddam. And the Negronis certainly helped.

After I explain all this to the bus driver he says, "You're not in the Vatican, ma'am. You're in BC. God's country. I personally guarantee that your bag will arrive safely. Watcha go to Italy for anyways? And where are ya heading?"

"Rome was a personal matter. I happen to be a native British Columbian. A Madigan," I inform him. "I've got to dress well for our Centennial Celebration. I'm going back home to Kettle Valley."

"Kettle Valley, eh? Madigan. Get on."

Being a senior with preferred status I grab a window seat up in front. Although I trust the driver, I worry about baggage-handlers because I've packed my bronze plaque. I could always buy new clothes if the worst came to the worst, because I must look my best for the Centennial, but that plaque could never be replaced.

I should never have packed the precious bronze plaque presented to me when I retired from Jonathan Swift Community College. That plaque was my reward for ten years of teaching drama. Time just flew because I loved every minute of it, and after my second husband Vladmir passed away, I provided the drama department with the continuity it needed in the Stanislavsky Method, which Vlad pioneered in Canadian theatre.

Teaching drama kept me busy and in touch with young people, even if it wasn't the sort of theatre career my mother had dreamed of for me. Movies, Broadway. Hitch your wagon to a star, she'd said.

I realize now how she must have felt, because I admit my two girls were a disappointment to me, career-wise. It must have been Karl's German genes. Not a sign of artistic temperament in either of them in spite of the cultural milieu of our home, and the way Vlad treated them as his own. Olga went into Phys Ed, Masha into marine biology. Poor Masha, to hell-and-gone out there in Newfoundland. Still a foreign country to my way of thinking, although quaint, like Ireland. Mind you, Olga got me started jogging, which kept me fit. That lady doctor at my last check-up said I had the heart and lungs of an eighteen-year-old. Of course I must give Mother part of the credit for that, teaching me deep-breathing in her elocution classes. I did follow through with a dramatic career, in a way.

I'd just die if I lost that plaque! I want to show it to all my school chums. Those who are left. Poor Janet Hughes died last year and Mary Ann is in the Boundary Nursing home. Alzheimer's, poor dear. They say that she was never the same after Peter's death. The shock. I'm lucky I'm so resilient, bouncing back the way I did after Vlad passed away.

I adjust the recliner and lean back in my seat, overwhelmed by fatigue. And fear. I took my own blood pressure at one of those machines in the pharmacy before leaving Toronto, and just thinking about this trip got it up to 150 over 120 — unusual for me. My blood pressure has always been low, I'm sure as a result of dance training. I had chest pains before I left, too, and although I was worried about these symptoms, I was afraid if I consulted the doctor she'd either make me stay home or tell me it was just mental. She's a young doctor, that Dr Parr. They're all young these days. The last time I went for surgery with an ankle fracture the emergency room looked as though it was being run by children. The male interns had long hair; the women short. It was hard to tell who was what.

They're all big on calling everything mental, these days, those young doctors. Mind you, I always preferred men doctors because they're more sympathetic. But that Dr Parr's office is right across from my apartment, so it saves travel. I do resent the way she calls me 'Jenny,' as if I were her contemporary, but I'm reluctant to correct her. Even though I'm exuberantly healthy, it's nice that she's nearby.

Right now my feet hurt from lengthy travelling. I slip off my shoes, turn my ankles in circles to keep them from swelling the way they did coming out on the plane.

---

We pass the Fraser, Langley, Mission. Lush to watch for a while, but this is not my personal landscape, even though it's almost as green as Ireland. I doze off.

The bus stops, lurching me awake. A passenger gets on.

I sit up to look around. There's been a long winter, because the higher mountains are still snow-covered. Real sky-piercing BC mountains. This is more like it.

I crane my neck, searching for familiar landmarks. Everything is less familiar to me now because of recent highway route changes, and because in the past I'd always taken the train. The Kettle Valley line no longer runs. Those bloody Feds are cutting back on everything.

As I watch, I can tell that the harsh drawn-out winter that

I'd read they had here in BC last year made everything greener. It's usually dry at this time of the summer.

"I'm stopping for a smoke," the driver says, "if anyone wants to get out for a five-minute break."

I grab my purse. When I stand up my knees stiffen. When I make it, I push towards the front where the driver helps me down. Stairs are hard on knees, I find. If it weren't for that, no one would ever guess my real age. 'It's how one moves that tells,' I always told my students. 'Let your gestures reveal character.'

Oh! The air is wonderful! I stand outside just breathing and gazing up at the mountains. I'm wearing running shoes, so can't resist sprinting past the coffee stop and around the bus. I'm panting when I get back, but my knees have loosened up and I feel superior again. Especially when I follow those hacking smokers aboard.

All my fears about this trip have vanished. I struggle to remember those lines from the Psalms, something about lifting up my eyes 'to the hills from whence cometh my strength.' It does! It does!

When the bus starts again I drink one of my juice cartons and look out on BC's sertão on our way to Osoyoos; observe land growing more lush as we pass through mining and logging terrain near Bridesville. Bridesville — what a name! Why did I never find out why it was called Bridesville? What bride came here? Why? How?

———

Then I see it. The Kettle River, coursing through Rock Creek. I'm home! It's *my* river, surging with melting snow that streams down mountain gullies. I rise from my seat and my eyes brim. This is my natal landscape: those are my mountains, purple at a distance. In autumn, russet; in spring, green with foliage.

At Midway we get off for coffee. I'm astonished that what was once a railway whistle-stop is now a prosperous town. In the bus-station I wonder whether to buy my grandson a T-shirt that reads, WHERE THE HELL IS ROCK CREEK BC? Instead, I buy bottled water and a hamburger. Some teenage back packers get on, laughing. They cluster together in seats at the rear as the bus starts up.

I enjoy the comfort of the bus, but remember those wonderful long trips I used to take on the old Kettle Valley line. Travelling to UBC and back; to musical festivals in Trail and Nelson. I used to buy treats from the newsie to quell hunger until I got home. How I loved that voyage! I smile, remembering what we called dining-car stewed prunes. 'CPR strawberries.'

---

The bus slows down and stops at Greenwood — a city saved from being a ghost town by the Japanese who were forced to come there as prisoners-of-war. Doctors, accountants, fishermen, torn from their west coast homes. They settled down and turned Greenwood into a thriving community even though everything they had owned was seized by our government. There were other groups, sent to New Denver, Kaslo, and Slocan, in the Kootenays.

Karl, my first husband was German, and his grandfather actually supported the enemy in the First World War. How come nobody confiscated his father's home?

I remember how suspicious we all were when we went to meet trains bringing the Japanese to Kettle Valley. We were like people going to see the circus come to town, staring at them. Their solemn faces peered back from the train windows. Silent, cautious.

At first, local citizens were curious. Then they grew resentful. Secret meetings were organized to drive 'the Japs' out of town, to keep them out of 'our' schools. As I think about it now, it comes close to the way the Ku Klux Klan operates. There was even a movement to make sure no 'Japs' could move inside the city limits of our beloved Kettle Valley. Thank God, Doctor Horne's wisdom prevailed. In those days, in small towns, doctors were the ultimate source of power. After Doctor Horne's outraged veto, the meetings stopped. The Japanese were allowed to attend our schools. There they earned more abuse because they were so bright and studious that they provided serious competition to us slackers. I did find myself less a loner after I met a kindred soul named Sumi, who was another bookworm. Today, she's still my best friend. With shame I recall that back in those early years, although she was my best friend at school, she was never invited to our home or to parties. We only entertained other 'whites.' That's how we actually spoke because that's how it was, then. The war, people said. Local women enjoyed discussing their new 'Jap' maids who were paid fifteen dollars a month. Young Japanese women, high school educated.

I take out the yellowed clipping I saved all these years, the one from *The Courier* describing the Golden Jubilee Pageant, a clipping I treasured because I thought it would be fun to show around. Upon re-reading, I find myself horrified by references to Japanese dancers. 'Kimonos and twirling parasols.' An Anglo-Canadian idea of their culture. What about the *noh* players, *kabuki*, or even martial arts exhibitions? Why had the Japanese even been gracious enough to participate?

Sumi hadn't, except in the background, and now I understand why. She realized that her people were being carica-
tured.

History has absolved them, as Fidel would say. Sumi is
now married to the district Member of Parliament. He's a
scholar, not given to the corny histrionics I remembered in
some of the Valley's earlier politicians.

We pass through Eholt where Mother's stepfather owned
saloons long ago, and where my older brothers, Fred and
Ken, were born in an early homestead. My dad and brothers
took me to Eholt once to visit Mrs Kelley, its sole inhabitant.
She was an Irish woman who kept goats, lived on home
brew, and walked all the way into town to buy her groceries.
Someone always drove her back home, sure of a mug of her
potent brew. Mother usually invited her in for a cup of tea, a
rest, and a talk about the early days. Mom made sure I was
shooed away. Eavesdropping, I learned why. Mrs Kelley's
language was as rich and lewd as The Wyf of Bathe. Local
wives were not too happy, if their husbands drove her home.
I think now that she met other needs than her drivers' thirst.

———————

Nearer Kettle Valley I see Galena Mountain at my right,
Rattlesnake Mountain straight ahead. When I was small I
wasn't allowed to cross the bridge because of rattlesnakes. I
didn't want to, after Fred stopped his Model-T to show me
their squished bodies on the lake road. Some of the kids even
collected rattles.

There was a man called Rattlesnake Bill who gathered
venom for the provincial lab. As a sideline to his venom
business, he made and collected violins. He sold one to my
mother. Usually Dad put up a fight when Mother made these

cultural purchases to enrich our Depression era life, but Rattlesnake Bill told her that this particular violin was a genuine Stradivarius. She paid fifteen dollars for it. Dad never complained, because he saw it as an investment. Nobody in our family ever learned to play it, but we always liked bringing it out to show people. It gave us a sense of security and prestige.

In the distance I see Observation Mountain which I climbed every Saturday during high school years. It was the one place we could be alone, as teenagers, to discuss boys, what little any of us knew about sex, and how we really felt about our parents. We sneaked out a copy of *Gone With the Wind* and read it up there, poring over the juicy bits. Phoebe's mother belonged to the Book-of-the-Month club.

---

I ask the driver if I may get out when we arrive at what was once called Doukhobor Hill, but the bus cannot make a stop. I used to bike out here to visit the wonderful brick houses with their big verandahs. That was in the old days of communal living: of shared kitchens and steambaths.

Near this region long ago, I'd seen barefoot women, pulling ploughs through the rich soil. That, I think, was true feminine power, although I was glad that later, Doukhobors prospered enough to buy horses to do this work.

We used to buy wood for our furnace from Mike Degraeff, a dear old man who delivered it in his horse-drawn wagon. Mother let me go out to talk to him while he unloaded. After he finished he'd sit me up in the front of the wagon beside him, drive around the alley and back to our front door. I felt just like the queen in her landau, waving grandly at our neighbours as we passed.

I'm saddened, knowing that the original Doukhobor community is gone. There are only token museums, one here another in Fructova. But I'm pleased that their wonderful choir put Kettle Valley on the map with their concert tours and CBC broadcasts. Doukhobor. The word means 'Spirit Wrestler.' Is that what I've been doing all my life? Wrestling my spirit? I remember being one of the few parents who was not shocked by young people forming communes in the sixties. 'What's the fuss about?' I told my friends. 'I grew up with people like that. They believe in what they called toil and peaceful living.'

Many Doukhobors intermarried, and most, like the Japanese, have become active in the larger community.

Not so, with dear placid Annie Sookocheff. During that big provincial government push — I forget whether it was the sixties or the seventies — to force Sons of Freedom children into 'English' schools when parents refused to enrol them, government social workers and the Mounties just came and removed them, placing them in the former Japanese camps in New Denver. Annie, like most mothers, was distraught by the separation and became an activist. I even read about her in the papers Back East, after she was imprisoned in Okhalla, where she led other parents in a hunger strike. Once she nearly died, until Dr Ryan flew down to persuade her to let him put her on an I.V. All those fasts and heartaches took their toll, though, and the strong young nurse I remember died in prison before her children were ever sent home. Her two sons have become environmentalists, and were jailed over logging protests on Vancouver

Island. All various governments ever succeeded in doing, with the Sons, in my opinion, was to keep creating new generations of activists.

What had all the fuss been about, really? My mother wasn't jailed for keeping me out of school for a year. I was supposed to be recovering from whooping cough, and spent a year competing in elocution contests in festivals all over BC. And of course now, 'home study' is very trendy with baby boomers who don't want their precious offspring in ordinary schools.

I wrote to Annie several times both before and after her imprisonment, but she never replied. I know she read and wrote in English, because she did at the hospital. It must have had something to do with the government running the Post Offices. I hope that was it. I'd hate to think it was because she decided I was one of Them. 'White.'

How come the mountains look closer than I remember? Oh, they just seem that way because the area has been built up so much, filling in what were once wild fields. Such a pity. Even up here in what used to be the barren West End there are stores, motels and big new homes.

I can't recognize those schools. Everything looks so strange and modern. I don't even know where the bus stop is now. Pete's brother-in-law, Roy, May's husband, promised to meet me, and booked me a place in one of the new motels. I tried to stay at the Province Hotel but the operator laughed when I phoned long distance. She told me it burned down years ago. Sumi phoned to arrange to meet me for lunch. As the MP's wife, naturally she has a lot of official functions to

attend, but she's always been loyal, kept in touch, made time
for me, and still regards me as her 'best friend.'
We pass the courthouse. It looks just the same. I squint
through my glasses, searching for the hospital where I used
to work in the summers. When I ask the driver about the
hospital, he tells me that it's been moved up to the West End.
There's the bus-stop! Who's that elderly couple? It can't
be May and Roy... they look much too old! *Dear God*, it is! I
stand waving at them out the window before the bus even
stops, and push my way down the aisle.

My motel is comfortable, in a whole new area on the other
side of the river from the city. It is operated by newcomers. I
didn't recognize their faces or their names and they didn't
recognize mine. That's surprising, them not recognizing
mine. And quite appalling after all my mother did for this
community. That was the main reason I kept the Madigan
name, a custom unheard of when I married, and which was
infuriating to Karl and his family. The German patriarchs,
the Pfeiffers.

This motel is on the once-forbidden side, right across
from Rattlesnake Mountain. Roy says the rattlesnakes have
moved into town now, so there's no 'safe' side of the river
anymore. It's pleasant out here, and I'm glad I'm on my own.
That is, *alone*. I need to explore and reminisce, to go where the
spirit moves me.

I shower, change, and stride into the dining room where
I order a meal of borsch, vareniki, and salad. Borsch, a
Doukhobor delicacy we once ridiculed along with other
Doukhobor dishes, has become a regional specialty which
outsiders drive into Kettle Valley to enjoy. It's not as good as

the borsch I remember choir members bringing my mother after the Golden Jubilee, but to me it's worth every cabbage leaf in nostalgia. The vareniki are stuffed with cottage cheese, potato, and swim in melted butter! Wonderful! Who cares about the cholesterol count!

I can't for the life of me figure out which wine would be appropriate for Doukhobor dining, as I read the menu. I'm not up to vodka, so settle on an Okanagan Estate dry white, a half-litre, which I really need after that long dry bus trip. Wine is good for the heart, they say, now. I'm glad I have new bifocals so I can read the menu without having to change my glasses.

I'm sad, after finishing my wonderful meal, remembering again my co-worker Annie. She's probably buried in a Sons of Freedom burial ground somewhere. There will be flowers, food, and pictures on her grave. I know I've kept a picture I treasure still. I took a snapshot of her once when she brought her new son for me to see. He was a darling, but I was surprised that she'd worn, not the traditional shawl and dress she wore after her marriage, but the same suit she used to wear to and from work at the hospital.

---

The girls won't be coming in from Back East until tomorrow, complete with their husbands and my grandchildren. 'The whole catastrophe,' as Zorba put it. I know they're making this effort to come, because 'mother is getting on.' I loathe the way they treat me. Patronizing. As if I'm in my dotage. I'll only have this evening and tomorrow morning to myself, and intend to make the most of it.

I did enjoy that Russian meal. Especially the piroshki for dessert, in which I recognized the flavour of our Valley plums. And I do have to admit that these local wines are as good as anything I ever drank in Rome or Paris. I pay with plastic, tip the waitress and leave.

I pass through a nearby park area filled with RV's and double-decker trailers that seem so popular in BC. All the motels and hotels, Roy said, were booked over a year ago. Local residents are entertaining friends from the old days and even opening their homes to visitors.

I haven't phoned May yet, although it was sweet of her and Roy to meet me. My encounter with them was so emotional that I'm still over-stimulated, and because I'm tearful, missing those who will never come back here again. Peter, Fred, Ken, Madge. And on and bloody on.

I know I'll have to visit the cemetery — I need to — but that can wait until the kids arrive. Flowers for their ancestors, et cetera. At least having the kids around acts as a sort of buffer. I put up this phony wall when I'm with them, to make life easier. It's too soon for me to get emotional again. I want, like Garbo, just to be alone.

---

I can't bear to think about visiting our dear family home without the kids, though. That's when I'll really need them. The last time I visited — it must have been in the fifties, because the girls were toddlers — left me feeling so *injured*. I had wanted to show them the fruit trees Daddy planted for each of his children. Three apple trees for the boys, a pear tree for Madge, and a plum tree for me. On that visit I dragged the girls out of the hotel, telling them again about how my father had taken each of us out to see our very own tree when it bloomed, and when its first fruit appeared, and how I was taking them see Mommy's special tree.

When we arrived at the house — I'd phoned the owners for permission to view the garden — the apple and pear trees were there, but my special plum tree had been chopped down. I was so distraught that I flung myself on the stump and sobbed. Masha and Irina started crying too because they didn't understand. When I tried to explain — I was hysterical, I know — they both grasped that the new owners' cruelty had done this to me. They picked up rocks and threw them at the windows. I didn't stop them. I was proud of them.

Roy told me that the present owners are a sweet young couple who have kept the caragana trees at the back, and that they wanted to meet me to learn more about our family. But now, over the acre lot that had once been the garden that fed us during the depression, has been built a huge house. Those wretched owners — the tree murderers — subdivided and sold out. What else could we have expected from newcomers with no sense of history? They were from Back East, I believe.

---

I stroll along the Kettle in a newly developed area that was once wilderness. I wonder if the residents of that charming cottage over there know that they live on grounds where once dwelt Mouldy Mike?

I'd forgotten all about him. He was a filthy old man who shared a shack with his goats and never crossed the bridge into town. Lived on goat's milk and what his garden produced. He was a mystery to us all, but the stench from his shack was enough to keep away the curious. He was an eccentric in days when we never saw people as being eccentric. We took people as they were. We just thought of him as Mouldy Mike. We were curious of course, but at that time there were too many other things to worry about. The Depression, the War. It was not until long after I'd married and left home that I learned Mike's whole story. It came out after his death, when records had to be obtained for registration and so forth. There was a big write-up in *The Courier*, about how he'd been an RCMP officer Back East, and after being jilted by his fiancee, gave up on everything, rode the rails west, and bought his goats. That was it. So romantic and Faulknerian. Nowadays, I suppose he'd be referred to some group for people undergoing separation trauma.

If only Phoebe had turned her mind to serious literature she could have written about all this folklore, instead of making a mint out of those trashy romance novels.

Oh! I smell nicotiana, giving off night fragrance from the garden where Mike once lived.

Enough exploration here. I yearn for my special place, my own spot of the Kettle. While strolling there, I breathe air that seems even better than it was up in Hope. That's because it's lower down here in the valley, so there's more oxygen. I once had a lover who said he loved me because embracing me was like breathing fresh air. It must have been someone in Toronto. The air here is so invigorating I can't resist a slow jog across the bridge. But only because I feel like it, not because it's good for me.

---

How I remember coming to this river! So many times in tears, and before and after the Golden Jubilee, after what I thought was my great disgrace. It's laughable now. Being so worried about my own misbehaviour that I was unaware of what was going on under my very own eyes.

Mother's relationship to Ned Jacob became obvious enough to result in their late marriage. I was appalled and unforgiving at the time — my God, she was a grandmother! But I was relieved that her affair absolved me from my drunken transgression. I'd lived in terror of her finding out, and felt guilty for years. I suppose she lived with her own terror and guilt. How to tell daddy's little girl about *her* long-standing romance. Her relationship with Ned also explained what I felt was Terry's appalling lack of responsibility. He really should have held back on rye that night. I guess he knew about Mother's romance, and thought if I were blotto enough I wouldn't figure out what was going on. His way of protecting her, which was kind of him really. Too bad about old Terry. Madge never did marry him. After her transfer she was courted by a dentist. Several months after the Jubilee they came home for a big wedding before settling down in Nanaimo. They had twin sons, who still keep in touch with my girls.

---

I was delighted when Miss Sutherland and Dr Ryan married and created a regional theological scandal. Not just in the town, but in the whole Kootenay-Boundary district, even getting Anglican and Catholic bishops involved. I think the ceremony was RC. They always win.

I received an invitation to the wedding, but was pregnant with Masha, and not up to travelling. By then Karl was working as a comptroller for the Tories in Ontario, a good job for a left-brained German with a Commerce degree. But I was not one who took well to controls. We broke up during the sixties.

When I went back to university to take night courses I met Vladmir. My family called him 'the Bolshevik.' Vlad and

I were happy together, and he provided the girls with an artistic milieu. They adored him, and I guess my early start with the Doukhobors and my working relationship with Annie gave me a special rapport with Vlad.

---

I wonder whatever became of Keith? I learned after my wild adventure with him that he'd been engaged all along. No wonder he'd been so inhibited. It was a blessing nothing did happen between us. Looking back at him now, and comparing him to men I subsequently met, he seems to have been a dry stick. Mother wrote that he'd married and gone to Africa to teach. Something to do with the Columbo plan.

Mother must have been in her sixties all those years she was carrying on with Ned, so there's still hope for me. Not that I don't get chances. I do. But as a former drama professor of Jonathan Swift College, I have a certain community image to maintain. Once I decided my career was more important I stopped dreaming about finding a third partner, because when it comes to men I get obsessive and have no time for anything else. Life is short but art is long.

I wonder if there will be anyone here who actually remembers me from the Jubilee? I'm sure there will, perhaps even Keith. I can laugh about that crazy night, now. Perhaps we could both laugh together.

I've learned over and over again that what Fred told me was right. Fifty years from now, no one will even give a goddam.

Only the Kettle River will still be here, and rivers, so far as I know, have no memory.

I have. Why did I hate everything about Kettle Valley so much? Why was I so determined to get out of this little landlocked valley, this paradise, to see beyond those mountains? Just like those pathetic sisters dreaming of Moscow. In those days I felt so claustrophobic, in this green pocket.

Now, back in Toronto, I yearn for mountains. In that lovely half-waking state every morning, I have this recurring dream. I'm home, back here in my valley, near this river, and surrounded by these mountains.

———————

Even that short jog has tired my feet. I untie my Reeboks, take off my socks and wade in. The water is icy and jolting at first, but my poor old legs adapt. The blood shoots up my ankles, calves, thighs, like an electric shock. Wonderful!

There's no one here. Everyone else is out drinking and visiting. Why not? I strip off sweatshirt, slacks, and underclothes, toss them up on the bank and dive in.

The summer air is cool on my back, the moon shines silver on the Kettle.

Tonight I'll battle the current and cross that river once again.